CHEADLE

NEVER
EVER

Other books by Helena Pielichaty

Accidental Friends
Saturday Girl

And for younger readers

Clubbing Together
Clubbing Again
Clubbing Forever
Love, Simone xxx
Jade's Story
Vicious Circle
There's Only One Danny Ogle

Helena Pielichaty

NEVER EVER

OXFORD
UNIVERSITY PRESS

to
Hanya Liesel
without whom I'd be nothing
(her words not mine)

OXFORD
UNIVERSITY PRESS

Great Clarendon Street, Oxford OX2 6DP

Oxford University Press is a department of the University of Oxford.
It furthers the University's objective of excellence in research, scholarship,
and education by publishing worldwide in

Oxford   New York

Auckland   Cape Town   Dar es Salaam   Hong Kong   Karachi
Kuala Lumpur   Madrid   Melbourne   Mexico City   Nairobi
New Delhi   Shanghai   Taipei   Toronto

With offices in

Argentina   Austria   Brazil   Chile   Czech Republic   France   Greece
Guatemala   Hungary   Italy   Japan   Poland   Portugal   Singapore
South Korea   Switzerland   Thailand   Turkey   Ukraine   Vietnam

Oxford is a registered trade mark of Oxford University Press
in the UK and in certain other countries

British Library Cataloguing in Publication Data

Data available

ISBN: 978-0-19-275525-4

1 3 5 7 9 10 8 6 4 2

Printed in Great Britain by Cox and Wyman Ltd, Reading, Berkshire

Paper used in the production of this book is a natural, recyclable product made
from wood grown in sustainable forests. The manufacturing process conforms
to the environmental regulations of the country of origin.

1
ERIN

My mornings were not the same any more. Until two weeks ago, I'd had my own room, with sloping ceilings and open shelving, Magritte posters, and *privacy*. Now there's ten square feet of Aston Villa wallpaper and a tacky metal window to be shared with Georgia, the middle one. Annoyingly, Georgia couldn't share with Nina, the youngest, because the third bedroom here was so—what would an estate agent say?—so *compact*, the headboard had been sawn off to get Nina's bed into the room.

Today, Georgia was plaguing me with stupid questions. 'What's it like having a period?' she asked.

'Fantastic,' I told her, brushing my hair.

'Really?'

'Really. You don't stop laughing for four days—five if you're lucky.'

'Megan Weeks has started hers. She's allowed to get changed for Games in the stock cupboard.'

'Those are only *some* of the perks,' I replied, throwing down the brush and searching for my shoes. I got down on all fours and squinted beneath the bed, laddering my only pair of decent tights on the bare floorboards. '*Merde*,' I said under my breath.

'Do you use pads or tampons?' Georgia pursued.

'Neither. I stuff an old pair of socks in my pants and hope for the best,' I replied.

'No you don't! You use both. I've seen them.'

'Why ask, then?' I was getting mad now. I couldn't find my shoes and I'd got about five seconds before the bus arrived and my eleven-year-old sister was revealing things about me she has no right to know, and wouldn't know, if my stupid parents hadn't messed up and lost our house and made us move to this bum hole.

Apparently, though, I was lucky. According to my mother, we'd been fortunate to get a council house so quickly, especially one on the York Estate. The York Estate had a good reputation. It was well known people on this estate won competitions for 'best kept garden' and had a *zero tolerance policy* on vandalism. And we're even on The Close, with a grassy area to look out on, instead of being overlooked. It's quite nice, really.

Course it is. It's *quite nice* living in a house without a telephone so I can't talk to my friends when I feel like it. It's *quite nice* waiting at the bus stop with the Scrunchie Girls every morning staring wordlessly at you. It's *quite nice* being told 'you're very posh' in the newsagents when all you did was ask for some Tictacs.

You could say I was finding it hard to adjust.

'If you're looking for your shoes, they're downstairs,' Georgia eventually revealed. 'Dad was cleaning them last night.'

'Part of his community service order, was it?' I spat.

2

'What do you mean?'

'Nothing,' I said, knowing Mum would be livid if I explained, and left her to wallow in the luxury of our shared cell.

Downstairs, Mum was trying to convince six-year-old Nina porridge was good for her. 'It tastes of frogs' skin,' Nina moaned.

'Like it or lump it,' Mum replied. She glanced at me but I looked away. We'd had a corker of a row last night and I wasn't ready for eye contact yet. 'Cutting it fine again, Erin,' she said casually as I slipped into my well-polished footwear. I chose not to reply, and shrugged my way round the table towards the back door. I had to breathe in because the table's massive and takes up all the floor space. As I struggled past, I snagged my tights again on one of its bulbous legs. 'Great! My last decent pair! I don't know why you didn't auction this thing off with all the other stuff!' I snapped.

'You know full well why not, Erin,' Mum replied calmly.

'It's a special table, isn't it, Mum? That's why you mustn't spill Ribena on it or draw smiley faces using felt pens,' Nina informed us gravely.

Yeah, yeah; the table was special, the table was unique. It had been handed down through three generations on my mother's side. It was an heirloom, a reminder of better days, and I loved it, too, when I was in a good mood and had tights to spare.

'Got your dinner money?' Mum asked.

'Yes,' I sighed, already halfway through the back door.

'We'll talk tonight,' she said.

'Can't wait,' I replied with just the right amount of sarcasm before disappearing.

'Love you,' she called after me.

I didn't respond. It was probably the briefest conversation I'd ever had with her before school.

Like I said, my mornings weren't the same any more.

At the bus stop, the Scrunchie Girls stared vacuously ahead. They all looked alike, these slapperettes; died hair with bad root-jobs, the dead-ends all held fast by cheap Lycra scrunchie hairbands. One of them, Chantal Pickwell, is in my year, Year Ten; the others are Year Nines. I noticed Chantal (three scrunchies) had a huge love-bite on her neck, the size of a Ritz cracker, that she was showing off to the others. Our new headteacher, Mr Riddick, would be down on her like a ton of breeze-blocks if he saw it. Love-bites were definitely not part of his 'new vision' for Adams High.

The bus was late. I was dying to get to school but the bus was late and along came Liam Droy. Maybe, just maybe, moving could have been bearable, but when I discovered we were going to be living on The Close with *him*, I knew my life was over. Liam-I-may-be-thick-but-I-think-I'm-gorgeous Droy. Liam-I-will-wreck-your-lesson-but-I'm-a-laugh-aren't-I? Droy.

Liam-I've-just-come-back-from-Minorca-what-are-you-doing-here-Mackiness? Droy.

'What are you doing here, Mackiness?' he asked.

'Minding my own business,' I answered.

He grinned. His white teeth shone, enhanced by his mid-term, unauthorized tan. He is very, very good-looking in an obvious football star sort of way. Fortunately, having excellent taste, I'm immune. Katia, my best friend, wanted to have his babies.

'Wotcha, Chan,' he greeted her, 'nice neck.'

'Chan' blushed and covered her love-bite with her hand, as if she had only just remembered it was there. 'It was Tommo. We were just messing about.'

'I'll bet you were,' Liam replied meaningfully.

Ah, Tommo. Aka Thomas Boyle, best friend of Droy and fellow pain in the love-bitten neck. Both in my form. Lucky, lucky, lucky girl that I am. Sadly, Droy returned his attention to me and I cursed all forms of public transport. 'Come on, though, blondie, what *are* you doing here? It's a bit far from your end, isn't it?' he asked.

As if I'd reply after the blondie bit. Curse blonde hair. Curse Road Car Buses.

'She moved here the day after you went on 'oliday,' Chantal informed him on my behalf. 'Lives where the Walesbys were before they got evicted.' She glanced sourly at me before continuing. 'They've not been on the corporation list two minutes either, my mam says. Our Nicola would have loved that house but they won't give her a three bedroom with only one baby.'

5

Well, sor-ee for existing, Mrs Pickwell. I can assure you if I had my way 'your' Nicola could have it this minute. Droy laughed, as if reading my thoughts, and punched me in the arm. 'Welcome to my world!' he joked. I couldn't return his smile. I have seen *his* house—houses—numbers nine and ten. They were unbelievably awful—pond, gnomes, fake wishing well, fake Mediterranean shutters against diamond-studded UPVC windows—the full fake works.

I turned away and fixed my eyes on the row of shops opposite, preferring the sight of a dog peeing against a letter box to Suntan Boy. I heard Chantal ask if he'd be going to the 'Centre' that night. She tried to sound casual but you could tell she hoped he'd say 'yes'. I could feel all the other little Scrunchies pricking up their ears to hear God's Gift's reply. 'Might do, might not,' he concluded. There was a collective, oestrogen-laden sigh. Tomorrow, I'd be walking on to the next bus stop.

Gabriel was waiting for me as I arrived. At least this part of my morning hadn't changed. Gabriel always timed his walk to school so that he met me off the bus, then together we waited for everyone else. I have three very close friends—Katia Pulic and Hannah Brough, whom I've known since Primary School, and Gabriel Owens, who has hung out with us since Year Seven. We're very protective of Gabriel; he gets called Gayboy a lot because he knocks around with us instead of gobbing on pavements and smelling of BO like some of the moronic males at Adams High. He is not gay but he's definitely a bit of a victim. The fact that his mum, who's a vicar, buys his clothes second-hand doesn't help and I noticed he'd been experimenting with his side-burns again but thought it best not to comment. 'Have you had a phone installed yet?' he asked as we headed for the main entrance where Hannah was waiting.

'Negative.'

'I tried phoning that call box number—you know—the one on Newstead Road, where I phoned you last time?'

'Aha.'

'This bloke answered and tried to sell me some hash!'

'I hope you said no.'

'Well, duh!'

'Cos I can get it much cheaper.'

'So when *are* you getting one put in? It took me three hours to do my maths last night,' Gabriel moaned.

I just gave it to him straight. 'We're not, the Mackinesses are going to be the only family in the entire western world without a telephone.'

'You're kidding!'

'I wish. I had a massive row with Mum about it last night.'

Gabriel looked concerned. 'You and your mum never row.'

'Oh, don't we?' I muttered.

'What are you going to do?'

'Save up for a mobile.' One they wouldn't know about and therefore couldn't confiscate.

'Obvious solution, O Wise One.'

'I thought so.'

Trouble was, my pocket money had been halved until 'things sorted themselves out' too, but I couldn't tell anyone that. There are only so many embarrassing disclosures you can make in one day. Instead, I broke the news to Hannah that she would be in charge of steering Gabriel through his maths until further notice. She glanced away and sighed hard, prompting Gabriel to protest that he wasn't *that* bad.

Katia was waiting for me outside French. She grinned her big grin, braces glinting 'neath the subdued (i.e. broken) lighting of the corridor, then pounced. 'Ernie!' (She always calls me Ernie.) 'Is he back? Have you seen him? Have you asked him out for me yet?' she spouted.

No point pretending I didn't know who 'he' was. 'It was wonderful,' I said.

'What was?'

'Sex with Droy—it lasted all night, despite his jet lag. He says I'm the best lover he's ever had.' She kicked the back of my heel. 'Watch it,' I said, 'they've been polished.'

Best Friend leaned heavily against a poster of Mont St Michel and sighed like a Scrunchie. I tried not to notice that it looked as if castle turrets were sticking out of her head. 'To think you live within walking distance of him. How lucky is that? Do you think your mum'd adopt me? I'd be good.'

'Katia, he's a pig and a slime-ball,' I said.

She pondered for a second. 'I object to the term "slime-ball" but will accept pig because it's a well-known fact all good-looking blokes are pigs. When can I sleep over?'

'When your taste improves.'

'Bitch.'

'Cow.'

'Slapper.'

'Girls! Really! If you are going to insult each other outside my room do so in the appropriate way!' Mr Whitehead, our French teacher, instructed us.

Katia straightened to allow him to pass, the turrets disappearing into her hair. '*Vache!*' she continued.

'*Cochon.*'

'*Bouton visage.*'

'*Derrière plus grande!*'

'*Salope!*'

'That's much better.' Mr Whitehead nodded approvingly as he opened the classroom door.

I love French, and Mr Whitehead's ace. He makes lessons interesting by telling us stories and stupid anecdotes about what he got up to during his year as an impoverished student in Paris. For example, did you know that they'd cut Napoleon's syphilitic knob off and pickled it? After he'd died, of course. I haven't eaten gherkins since.

Today, though, we were actually doing some work. Mr Whitehead had apologized, explaining the Head expected it of top sets, so we agreed to the assignment *this* time, providing he didn't make a habit of it. I was well away, booking a twin room for three nights with breakfast and evening meal in l'hôtel de Ginola, when I felt Katia's leg bash into mine, followed by a strange gurgling sound coming from her throat.

I looked up to see Mme Crecy, the exchange teacher, gesticulating wildly to Mr Whitehead; her eyes brimming with tears, her face as pink as a summer pudding. Behind her, Droy and Boyle hung their heads, trying hard not to laugh in case more sawdust fell out. Mr Whitehead gave them a dead-eye and assured Madame he'd 'sort it'. He ordered them to sit in the only two spare places he had—right behind us. Katia's gurgling stopped abruptly, along with her breathing. I wondered exactly when I'd have to give her mouth-to-mouth.

'We meet again, Mackiness,' Droy-boy whispered. Mr Whitehead immediately slapped a detention slip in front of him, saving me the bother of a reply. *I can feel his breath on my neck*, Katia scribbled on her file paper. *Think yourself lucky you can't smell it*, I scribbled back, and returned to my work.

Mr Whitehead asked us to pack away early because he had an announcement to make. Immediately, he began dispensing handouts, talking as he walked along the rows. 'Owing to the mental instability of my department, we have decided to arrange a Year Ten trip to France next Easter. We'll be staying for five nights in a hostel in the medieval walled city of Combourg in Normandy. During our stay we will visit Bayeux, home of needlework, and venture to Paris for a day. Price is fully inclusive of everything, except money for drink and drugs, but places are limited so it's first come, first served. We'll need a deposit of fifty pounds as soon as possible to guarantee a place. And may the Lord have mercy on our souls.'

A trip to France! I wanted to go so much but one glance at the price was enough to make my heart sink.

'Seriously though, this trip will be particularly useful for practising your oral and aural skills before next year's exam, especially those of you wanting a good grade to go on to do A/S level,' Mr Whitehead continued.

'That means us, Ernie,' Katia said. 'Are we going?'

'It depends,' I replied.

Mr Whitehead, who must have been standing behind us, leaned down and said, 'You'd better be going, Erin, I need at least some students with me who won't show me up!'

I folded the handout neatly and slid it into my planner.

'I wonder why he never said that to us?' Tommo wisecracked as we all rose to leave.

At lunchtime we joined up with Hannah and Gabriel in the dining hall. They'd had the same details from Mme Crecy and said they were definitely going on the trip. It was all right for them. Hannah had infinite guilt-money from her dad (your classic case of 'I'm sorry I ran off and left you all, darling; have a pony' parenting). Gabriel was more of the 'our son needs all the help he can get when it comes to education, where do we sign?' variety.

'How come Liam and Tommy were kicked out of your lesson?' Katia asked them. It never took her long to bring the subject round to *him*.

Hannah rolled her eyes. 'They just know how to wind her up,' she said dully.

'They sat behind us,' Katia said dreamily, trying to get a chip in her mouth and missing. 'I could feel Liam's breath on my neck.'

'Oh, for God's sake, haven't you anything better to think about?' Hannah snapped.

We stared at her. Hannah Beverley Brough never snaps. She's Miss Placid. She reads Jane Austen. She saves whales. She does not snap. 'What's wrong?' Katia asked.

Hannah lowered her eyes. 'It's my mum, she's found a lump on her breast.'

'Oh no,' Katia whispered.

'She's going to the hospital for tests today. I wanted to go with her but she wouldn't let me. What if it's cancer? What if she dies?'

'She won't,' I said, trying to reassure her.

Hannah looked at me, her eyes glittering. 'Sophie and me would have to go and stay with Dad in that stupid barn conversion and live with that stupid cow he's shacked up with. I'd rather kill myself.'

Gabriel put his arms around Hannah's shoulders, hugging her. 'Your mum'll be fine,' he told her.

2

Hannah's distress made me think about my mum on the way home; how I'd frozen her out this morning, not said 'Love you, too,' as I usually did, just because of a stupid telephone. What if *she* found a lump on her breast? Or what if she was already dead? Killed in a road accident taking Georgia and Nina to school? There were some crappy junctions on the road into town, she was always saying so. I could see her flying through the windscreen, her head smashed to a pulp like a ripe tomato. Tears pricked my eyes as I began to plan the funeral. I'd have to organize everything because Dad would be too distraught. Burial or cremation? Flowers or wreaths or both or neither? Which songs? Her favourite was 'Perfect Day'. Not appropriate.

I was so lost in my morbid thoughts, I didn't notice Droy-boy plonking himself down next to me until it was too late. 'Now then, blondie,' he greeted me.

I sighed peevishly. Yes, Liam, I still have blonde hair, just like I did this morning. Yes, it is natural. No, I do not want to be a Breakfast TV presenter. How to put this message across as simply as possible? 'Bog off,' I replied.

'Tch! That's no way to greet a neighbour.'

'I might live near you, it doesn't mean I have to talk to you,' I barked. Couldn't he see I had things on my mind?

'Why *wouldn't* you talk to me?' he asked. He sounded hurt.

I glanced at him. He was looking at me inquisitively, the green eyes Katia dreamed about open and expectant.

'Forget it,' I said.

'I can't believe you're on The Close.'

'Why shouldn't I be?' I said defensively.

'It's just weird, like the queen moving into Coronation Street.'

'Yeah, right. It's just like that. Shouldn't you be kneeling?'

'How come, though? Chantal says your dad's been sent down but Tommo says he's seen him—he reckons you're doing *Lifeswaps*.'

I laughed out loud. 'I wish,' I said. *Lifeswaps* was one of those BBC documentaries where families from different backgrounds exchange lives for a month—houses, incomes, social life—the lot. One wealthy woman from Yorkshire had fainted when she realized she'd only have one bathroom and would have to drive a T-reg Astra.

The Droy elbowed me again. Once more and I'd have him beheaded. 'Come on, then, tell me. You might as well, I'll only find out later from my mam.'

'Your mum?'

'Mrs Nosygit; she'll be wrecked when she discovers a new family's moved in without her being there. I bet

14

you ten quid she's been round to yours already. She'll know your date of birth, how much you weighed when you were born, and what you had for breakfast this time last year.'

'God,' I said, twisting round to look out of the window.

'Go on,' he urged, 'tell me.'

What happened was very boring, and, I guess, not that unusual. About ten years ago, after my dad, Noel, had been made redundant from his teaching post and when everyone thought *a mouse pad* was a hole in the skirting board, he had set up in business with his best friend, Steve Rawlinson, selling computers. Steve had invested capital but Dad had invested our house, The Lodge, in Greenway Park, as security. Dad did all the promotions and 'people' side and Steve sorted out the accounts—or so we thought.

At first everything was doing great and there were jokes about retiring to the Maldives etc. Then everyone set up computer outlets and the jokes stopped. Steve started to make cutbacks, like not paying taxes and VAT. Strangely enough, this was spotted, and Mr Taxman and Mr Vatman took M&R Computers to court. Mr Judge took away our house and gave Noel and Steve community service for being naughty boys. Noel and Steve had a big fall out and Steve moved to Leicester and we moved to The Close but no one lived happily ever after.

Dad's still doing his community service—two hundred hours of painting and decorating the youth and community centres in town. The theory is he's going to find another job as soon as he's finished and we'll be able to start again. 'All this is only temporary, Erin,' Mum had promised when we looked round the house on The Close. But I'd seen the changes in Dad, the way he closed himself off from all of us when he came home, the way he either gazed blankly or shouted at Mum when she put the Jobs page out for him. No way was 'this' only temporary. Not that I was going to tell Liam Droy that.

He nudged me in the arm. 'I'll show you round if you like,' he offered.

'Around where?'

'Everywhere. Introduce you to everyone, take you to the Centre.'

'No thanks.'

'Why not?'

For some reason—I don't know—maybe the 'queen' bit giving me ideas, I found myself putting on a snobby accent. 'I doubt that I'll have anything in common with anyone. No offence.'

'Suit yourself.'

We sat in silence for a while. I wished he would go upstairs to sit with the Scrunchies and the smokers. I wondered why he hadn't. 'Are you going on the French trip?' he asked.

'I haven't decided,' I mumbled.

'I am. A week off school, chatting up French birds. Try and stop me.'

'Can you afford it?' I asked, voicing my own worries out loud but still in that fake posh voice.

16

Liam bridled. 'Sorry,' I said, returning to normal, 'that didn't come out the way I meant it.'

'No, I bet it didn't,' he scoffed.

I got my wish. Liam sloped off to the upper deck and I was left on my own.

'Don't you know he's loaded?' a voice said from behind. I turned to see one of the Year Nines (double-scrunchie, nose-stud) from this morning staring at me.

'So?' I shrugged.

The girl continued anyway, squelching gum as she talked. 'His dad, Tony, owns all the Pine Island shops. My dad works for him.'

'Super,' I said, hoping that would be an end to it.

'My dad says unemployment on the estate'd double if it wasn't for Tony Droy.'

'Fascinating.'

'You should show Liam more respect,' she said tartly.

That did it. I reached up and rang the bell for the next stop. I was half a mile too early but a final straw's a final straw.

I was in such a strop by the time I got home, I forgot to be relieved at the sight of my mother, alive and well and painting the kitchen window. Slamming my bag down on the table, I asked what time dinner would be ready. Mum didn't turn round. She was in a precarious position, kneeling on the worktop, trying not to fall into the sink. 'It'll be ready when you've made it. Hello to you, too.'

'When I've made it?' I asked in disbelief. Had she felt the weight of homework in my bag?

She still didn't turn round. 'I want to finish this. If I stop now I'll have to wash the brush out and I've hardly any turps left. It doesn't have to be anything special; chicken dippers and oven chips will do.'

That was it, then. We'd turned into a chicken dippers and oven chips mid-week, not just Fridays, family. I couldn't remember the last time we'd had something home baked and wholesome. It was all: 'get the economy brand' and: 'put those back, we can't afford them' when we shopped now.

I couldn't stand it. 'Can I go phone Hannah first?' I pleaded.

She sighed heavily, her shoulders drooping from somewhere within Dad's old denim shirt. 'Can't it wait two minutes? You've been with her all day and the girls are hungry.'

'Even Georgia could do oven chips,' I pointed out.

'Georgia could, but I've asked you.'

'I won't be long. I promised I'd phone.'

Mum slapped some paint on to the sill. 'Go,' she said, 'just bloody go.'

I registered the 'bloody'. Chicken dippers, oven chips, and a foul-mouthed mother. The slippery slope. I bloody went.

There's a double payphone on Newstead Road. I liked the one facing away from the road because I could see fields and woods behind the house roofs. It reminded me that there was another world out there, away from the empty cans of Coke at my feet. I gazed at the fields as I waited for Hannah to answer but I just got the engaged tone all the time. I tried Katia, who told me she'd heard Mrs Brough's tests had gone OK but she would have to wait two weeks for the results. We both agreed we'd hate to wait that long and then chinned about other stuff until I'd run out of money and had to go back to The Close. I felt better after my talk with Katia, though; more sociable.

'OK, Miss *Can't Cook Won't Cook*'s here,' I announced on my return.

Mum was slamming the oven door shut. 'Don't bother, I'll do it,' she said off-handedly.

I glanced across at the window frame, half shiny white, half tobacco yellow. The brush was upended in a jam jar nearby, immersed in half an inch of cloudy liquid. 'You don't have to,' I said.

'Peas or beans?' she asked through gritted teeth.

'Whatever's easier,' I replied, not flinching. You must never give in when they're guilt-tripping you.

'Peas it is, then.' In one swift movement she swivelled round and opened the freezer compartment, grabbed the Bird's Eyes and slammed the freezer door shut again. I put my hands on my hips and looked down at her over my imaginary varifocals. 'Young lady, if you have to be bad tempered don't take it out on my oven. Do you know how long it took your father and I to save up for that Zanussi?'

My imitation of Dad's mum, Margaret, never failed. Finally Mum smiled, encouraging more mickey-taking.

'And what on earth have you done with your hair, Susan? You haven't had one of those tints on it, have you? Because you know you'll get alopecia, don't you? Remember Noel's Auntie Janet.'

Mum's hand automatically went to the bandana holding back her hair, patting it flat. I noticed her roots were showing, and looking nearly as bad as Chantal Pickwell's. Mum hated root growth, and it dawned on me she couldn't even afford to go to the hairdresser's now. It was then it hit me just how bad things were. We'd lost our house, we were on Income Support, and we couldn't afford a telephone but it took Mum's root growth to finally bring it home to me. As for going to France: I didn't have a rat's chance and, like Nina's porridge this morning, I could like it or lump it.

I looked closely at my mum's face for the first time in ages; saw how she actually looked forty now but never had before, saw the brave flicker of her smile betrayed by the hurt in her eyes. 'Seriously, Mum, I'll finish making the dinner,' I offered. It was all I could think of saying.

She shook her head. 'It's OK, I've started now. Get changed and then come and set the table. Tell Nina and Georgia to wash their hands.'

'I love you, Mum,' I said but kind of mumbling it under my breath. I think she heard but she'd already gone rummaging in one of the unloaded boxes for something and didn't reply.

Dad was working late, making it just the four of us for dinner. Georgia and Nina were wolfing down their meal as if they'd just ended a twenty-four hour fast for Oxfam. 'These are cool,' Nina said, gnawing at the edges of her last dipper, then sticking it in ketchup, before nibbling again. 'Can we have them tomorrow?'

'It's my turn to choose tomorrow. We're having spaghetti,' Georgia pointed out. 'Aren't we, Mum, we're having spaghetti?'

Mum pointed to her mouth, indicating she couldn't talk because it was full. She had almost finished her meal, ahead of even speedy-guts Georgia. That was another change; Mum had gained weight over the last few months and it was beginning to be noticeable round her chin and hips and stomach. She'd taken to wearing baggy shirts and jogging bottoms all the time. Not that it mattered, it was just not like her. Dad had done the opposite—he'd lost weight, so that his trousers hung baggily round his bum and his neck had that scraggy turkey look.

'Hannah's worried about her mum,' I revealed, knowing I was free of Dad's *not-women's-things-please* look. 'She's found a lump in her breast.'

Mum's eyes filled with concern instantly. 'Oh, poor Mary. Has she been to the hospital?'

'She's been today to have it checked out. A biopsy or something?'

'Is a lump bad?' Georgia asked.

'Course it is!' I replied sharply. 'Why don't you go watch TV?' I wanted to be alone with Mum for once, to talk properly to her, without sisters and dads butting in.

'Why is it bad?' Georgia pursued.

'It's not something you need to know about,' I said.

Mum leaned across, gathering the empty plates. 'It's not necessarily bad news. Often lumps are just cysts or bits of fatty tissue that go away or can be taken out.'

'Taken out?' Georgia persisted.

'By a doctor,' Mum added.

'With a big, rusty carving knife,' I drooled.

That got rid of her. Middle sister slid from her chair and legged it, knocking her glass of squash over the table as she did so. Immediate red alert. Nina passed the dishcloth to Mum, then scarpered. Mum began dabbing furiously at the orange liquid as it escaped in all directions over the precious heirloom's surface. Of course it was me who got it in the neck. 'I wish you wouldn't tease Georgia, Erin. She's growing up too, you know—you could take her a little more seriously,' Mum snapped.

'OK, OK, I'll go talk to her.'

She dabbed away without looking at me, mumbling about the table being 'the only decent thing we'd got'. I suppose that was my fault, too.

Upstairs, Georgia was face down on top of her bed, bawling her eyes out. I sat down next to her, trying to lift her arm away from her face but she told me to get lost. 'Come on, Georgy, this is a bit over the top, isn't it?'

She cried harder, her shoulders heaving up and down. 'I was only kidding about the knife,' I said.

'Look, you've read enough *Point Horrors* not to be scared of comments like that.' I stroked her hair, like I used to when she had nightmares.

'I've got lumps,' she said.

'What do you mean?'

'In my bosoms. I've got lumps.'

I tried not to laugh at her use of the word 'bosoms' and asked her again what she meant. She sat up, sniffing back her tears, and pointed to her chest. 'They don't hurt or anything but they're definitely lumps. Am I going to die like Hannah's mum?'

'No,' I said, as it dawned on me what she meant. 'It just means you're developing. Do the lumps feel like little grapes behind your nipples?'

'Yes.'

'That's normal, I promise. You're growing up.'

The relief on her face was tremendous, poor kid. Mum was right; I had to start treating Georgia with a bit of respect, especially if we were sharing a room. 'You'll probably start your periods soon,' I said to cheer her up.

She frowned. 'I don't want to, it looks too messy. I wouldn't mind wearing a bra, though. Megan Weeks wears a Wonderbra.'

'No, she doesn't.'

'She does!'

'Listen, sis,' I said, getting into this older/wiser sibling-role, 'if you want to know anything, just ask me, not Megan Weeks, OK?'

'OK,' she said, shuffling up and smiling, 'what's a dildo?'

23

3

'So what did you say to her?' Katia laughed after I'd repeated Georgia's question. We were waiting for Mr Whitehead to arrive for our lesson, first thing. She had the usual turrets sticking out of her head and I was trying to unknot the drawstrings of my bag without much success. 'Said there were some things even I didn't know yet and best to ask Mum.'

'Ooh, you likkle liar!' Katia teased. 'Eh, have you brought your money for the French trip?'

'Er . . . no. I forgot,' the likkle liar lied.

'I've got to save up half my own spend!' she said indignantly. 'And I have to buy Mum some Chanel perfume on the ferry. Talk about mean. She's pushing it, that woman.'

Another girl from our set, Becky, joined in. 'Yeah, I know. I've got to use a hundred pounds of my savings if I want to go.'

A lightbulb switched on in my head. Savings! I had savings. Somewhere, in a passbook, in The Important Papers/Where's the blinking passports? drawer in Mum and Dad's bedroom, I had savings. Money Grandad Alan had left me when he died. Money I wasn't supposed to touch, until I was eighteen and ready for college. But this was educational, wasn't it? And I'd still have loads left over.

I felt elated. Even the sight of Liam Droy, swaggering in with Tommo, joining top set under very false pretences until the end of term, couldn't burst my bubble. Not even when he slapped a cheque for the full whack in Mr Whitehead's hand, staring at me all the time as if to say *'Take that, you stuck-up tart'*.

'Any more deposits for the trip before I begin the lesson?' Mr Whitehead asked.

My hand shot up in the air. 'I'll bring mine by Friday,' I said loudly, mentally taking into account Mum going into town, withdrawing the cash, bringing it home etc. etc.

Mr Whitehead smiled, marking my name down on his list. 'At the latest, Erin,' he warned. 'Any more? What about you, Thomas? Aren't you joining your friend Liam?'

'Nah! Can't afford it—we're skint,' he said. There was a ripple of laughter round the room; not *at* him, but *with* him, for his openness. If I had to choose which one I'd rather be stuck in a lift with, Liam or Thomas, it would be Thomas. At least he had a brain. I remembered in Year Seven, when the class actually cared if we got merit marks or not, being neck and neck with him to be the first to achieve 'gold'. He beat me to it by delivering this tremendous speech in English about human rights and the teacher awarded him a record five merits in one hit. He had all the makings of a major boff-head but seemed to fade out in Year Eight and by Year Nine the conscientious Thomas Boyle had been replaced by the drongo Thomas Boyle one behind me. Punishment for hanging out with Droy, I guessed.

At lunchtime, still high from being able to participate in the trip like everyone else, I invited the gang over for 'chats' on Saturday. They hadn't been to The Close yet, and if I was honest, I was a bit embarrassed about them seeing the place but I supposed they'd have to visit at some stage, so I risked it.

'Don't expect anything like the old house, though,' I began defensively, 'it's miles smaller and I have to share with Georgia, so we might not get much privacy.'

'We don't care, Erin, it's you we want to see,' Hannah said. 'Anyway, it'll give me an excuse for getting out of the house. Mum's doing my head in with her I-don't-want-to-discuss-things routine. I mean, it's not as if she can pretend it's not happening, like when Dad was having his affair, is it?'

'Er . . . no,' I answered.

'Still no news from the hospital?' Gabriel asked.

Hannah shook her head and looked away, her eyes filling with instant tears. Wrong time, wrong place to talk. I wished I still lived near her, so I could drop in like I used to, or at least had a phone so I could call her up. Being poor sucked.

Katia linked her arm through Hannah's and changed

the subject. 'I've heard the youth centre on Newstead Road's really good on Saturdays. I think we ought to go, to help Ernie settle in and meet new people. You know how anti-social she is if she's left to her own devices.'

'And there's always a chance Liam might be there,' Hannah added, managing a faint smile.

Katia looked round, pretending to be offended. 'Did I mention him? Did I?'

I knew I'd have to be subtle when I asked for the money for France. Both Mum and Dad had always stressed how important the three thousand pounds was we had each inherited for our future. All I had to do was convince them the future had arrived.

I waited patiently for the signals that told me the time was right. Nina was already in bed, blissfully happy because I'd read to her; Georgia was in the bath, examining her lumps, no doubt. Mum was reading *The Chad* and Dad was sitting back, feet up, ready for the News.

The letter about the French trip lay neatly folded in my lap. I tapped it lightly, waiting, waiting until Dad eased back the ring-pull on his nightly can of beer and took his first sip, swallowed, rolled his eyes at the newscaster's gravely bad tie and . . . Action!

'Mum?'

'Mmm.'

I've got a letter here about a French trip next Easter.

Mr Whitehead said it was vital for anyone thinking of taking A/S level to go on it.'

Mum glanced up from her paper, immediately suspicious. 'Vital?'

'Well, not vital, exactly,' I conceded, 'but important. Can I go?'

She scratched the side of her nose, then held out her hand for the letter. I handed it across. 'Katia's going, and Hannah, and Gabriel,' I said, watching carefully as she skimmed the contents. Mum frowned. Knowing she had reached the cost, I leaped in with my cunning plan. 'I know it's expensive but we can pay in instalments over the six months . . . '

'It's not that, so much . . . '

'But what I thought was . . . '

Mum shook her head, staring at me apologetically. 'I'd love to say yes, Erin, you know I would, but you also know how things are at the moment. It's impossible.'

Dad proffered his hand. 'Let me see,' he said. He laughed sardonically and handed the letter back to Mum without comment.

'I thought I could use Grandad Alan's money,' I said hurriedly. 'I mean, the trip is educational and I do want to do A/S level and . . . '

Dad cleared his throat noisily and stared at the television while Mum seemed to be deeply engrossed in her shoes. Cue for pleading tone of angelic daughter. 'I really want to go, Mum,' I said. She looked at me, back at her shoes, then across to Dad.

Dad wiped his hand across his face. Always a bad

sign. Then, he got up and switched off the TV. An unprecedented sign. He stood up, hitching up his jeans awkwardly, and began rocking backwards and forwards on the balls of his feet. What the hell was he up to? He looked towards me but not directly into my eyes. 'I'm sorry, Erin, but . . . ' There was more rocking to and fro.

'But what?'

'We've had to use Grandad's money already. I was hoping you wouldn't need to know until I'd had a chance to pay it back. There'll be no French trip.'

I couldn't believe what I was hearing. That was my money. My money, left to me. 'Excuse me?' I asked in disbelief. 'You've what?'

Dad turned to Mum but she was still fully focused on her shoes. Coward. 'I had to, Erin. It was either that or lose the Espace,' Dad continued.

'Why my money?' I pounced. 'Why not Georgia's or Nina's? They're younger. They don't need it.'

'I've used theirs too,' he mumbled. 'We'd only just taken the loan out on the car and had to pay the balance off. It was over eight thousand.' Dad tried to look me in the eye, couldn't quite make it and his gaze landed somewhere left of my neck.

This was so, so unbelievable. I mean, how many times had they nagged me about not frittering money away and saving for the future? One million? Two million? I felt a cold anger swamp me. 'That was my inheritance! You'd no right to touch it.'

Dad took a defensive step back. 'It was either that

29

or the car and we can't live without a car. Not with five of us. Your mum and I had to think of the family as a whole.'

'We had no choice,' Mum whispered, running her hand nervously through her hair. The dark roots stood out even more this time but I didn't feel the previous surge of sympathy. This time I just saw them as a sign of failure.

'I hate you both,' I told them and ran out.

4
LIAM

Me and Erin are walking along a deserted Jamaican beach. We've got our arms round each other and I can feel the rise and fall of her hip-bone through the transparent sarong she's wearing. Erin smiles, her fantastic blonde, silky hair brushing gently around her face. 'Liam,' she moans, 'I want you.' I close my eyes and groan. It's enough.

I turn the shower on full-blast and begin to lather up with Oblivion for Men, knowing that my little soldier will be standing to attention any second, except that plan is shafted by my old man barging in. 'Liam, I'm using your lav, so stop playing with yourself,' he shouts, banging on the shower screen as he passes. Mind reader. Good job the screen's all steamed up.

''kin' hell, Dad!'

He doesn't answer. I can hear him, full flow like Niagara Falls, whistling some ancient Rod Stewart tune that drowns out my telly in the next room, never mind anything else. He then flushes *my* bog and starts staring into *my* mirror. 'Away then,' I complain, shoving my head round *my* en suite.

'Sorry, mate,' he says, taking his shaver from his

dressing gown pocket and plugging it in, 'your mother's Immacing her bikini line and there's only so much a man can take first thing.'

'More than I want to know!'

'I know,' Dad sighs, 'it's not a pretty sight.'

'You could wait till I've finished.'

'Yeah, I could,' he says, dead clever.

I switch off the shower and grab the towel from the rail opposite. No point staying in now.

In my room, I turn the TV up louder to drown out the drone from his shaver, then get dressed. I chuck my uniform on, hating every item. It stinks. It has no class, no style. Grey trousers, white shirt, claret and yellow tie. Claret and yellow, for chuff's sake! That new bloke Riddick has a lot to answer for. I glance outside. It's not raining so at least I can leave out the sweatshirt. All the better to show off your tan, you handsome dog.

My phone rings from the bedside cabinet. 'If that's Carver Street tell them I'll be there at half-past,' Dad shouts through. Radar ears. It's not Carver Street, where he's just opened his sixth shop, it's Chantal. Boring. Boring. I don't bother to lower the TV, even though it's the News.

'Is that you, Liam?'

'Who else is it going to be?'

She giggles, I wait. 'What do you want?' I ask.

'Nothing, really.'

'Then get off the line.'

She hesitates, stalling. I know she's bored—she'll have been up for hours, pushing her sister Nicole's baby, Morgan, round the shops until it stops crying. 'I just wondered if you'd got any suggestions for Tommo's birthday present,' she manages eventually.

'It's weeks away.' Four weeks to be precise. November the twenty-sixth. Same day as Dad's.

'I know, but, you know.'

'Just give him the same thing you gave him when I was on holiday—that'll keep him happy,' I reply.

'We never did anything, Liam, honest,' she says instantly but she's mistaken me for someone who gives a damn. She's desperate to play boyfriend-girlfriend with me but Chan's got a bad reputation and I don't want to date a bird who's seen as 'easy'—know what I mean? You've got to set standards. I don't object to having a quick grope outside the Centre on youth club nights, mind, and all right, maybe I do string her along a bit but it's all part of the act, isn't it?

'Listen, Chan, I'm starkers and it's freezing. Catch you later, OK?'

She agrees reluctantly. 'Yeah, OK, see you on the bus, yeah? I'll save you a place, yeah?'

I hang up, wishing I'd never given her my number. Dad walks through, rubbing a hand over his clean-shaven chops. 'And which of your little harem was that one?' he asked.

'Monday or Tuesday, I get them mixed up,' I reply.

He suddenly grabs me in a neck-lock. I struggle to get out of it but he's too strong and the more I struggle, the tighter his grip becomes. 'Get off!' I yell at him, almost puking from the whiff of his after-shave.

His voice comes over all serious. 'Just you be careful, Liam. I don't want you ending up one of those teenage fathers with two kids and a doormat wife before you're old enough to drink.'

'How will I?'

'Because I know the signs, clever dick.'

'What signs?' I bluster. Mum and Dad are both from travelling families; they take sex and marriage really seriously. The women have to be virgins when they get married, it's the rule, even these days, and even the lads have to think twice about where they're sowing the old seed. Talk about old-fashioned.

'What signs?' Dad continues. 'Girls phoning the house every two minutes. Blokes at work digging me in the ribs saying, "Your Liam's a right little charmer, got our so-and-so well hooked."'

'You did say "well *hooked*"?'

Dad wasn't amused. 'Look at me, son.'

I look. I see a smart bloke, young for his age. A guy without any hint of a beer gut or hair loss or bits sprouting from his ears and nose. A guy very difficult to take the mess out of, on a physical level. Just like me.

'What?' I ask, all innocent and non-melting butter.

'I am too young to be a grandad.'

'As if! I know what I'm doing.'

He snorts, letting me go. 'Oh, do you now? Well, just remember, there's Aids and all sorts out there. Make sure the three minutes is worth it.'

Crikey. It wasn't even eight o'clock in the morning

34

and I was being given the old birds and bees malarkey. 'What's brought this on?' I ask suspiciously.

'You just be careful with that Chantal—she's got "needy" written all over her. One wrong move and you'll be up that aisle before you know what's hit you—and knowing her mother, it'll be a baseball bat.' Pat Pickwell was fond of baseball bats, I admit. She knew just where to swing, as the poor sucker who denied fathering Morgan found out one dark night outside The Grey Horse.

'She's nothing to do with me,' I say, shuddering. 'Tommo was in there while we were in Minorca. It's Benny Ma Pickwell can go after.'

'Phh! Fat lot of good that'll do her,' Dad sniffs, like I knew he would. Tommo's dad had been one of his best joiners once but he'd blown it with the booze. Arriving smashed every morning, when he arrived at all. A real mess-up, for all his books about socialism and solidarity. Bit of a *Leftie* was Benny Boyle. Dad had been forced to sack him in the end. It had been a bit awkward between me and Tommo for a while, but we'd toughed it out. We go back too far to let anything like that come between us.

Mum shouts upstairs to say breakfast is ready. For once I rush down to eat it, leaving Dad to concentrate on other things instead of me.

Mum is sat down opposite me, pouring the tea, a sorrowful look on her face.

'What's up? Have you sprung a leak?' I joked, trying not to stare at her thrup'nnies which are sticking

35

out like two bowler hats on a walking stick. Most mothers ask for flowers or jewellery for their birthdays, don't they? Not mine. Implants. Thirty-eight years old. Thirty-eight inch hooters. It's sick. Especially as the rest of her doesn't exactly match. She's so skinny, with these thin little chicken legs, I keep waiting for her to keel over.

'Look,' she says, 'this has just arrived in the post and it's chipped.' She pulls back a layer of bubble wrap to reveal yet another Lady Diana limited edition, this one with a chunk out of her barnet.

'What do you need another plate for? You've got hundreds.'

'It's my hobby, Liam. Do I moan at your CD collection? No. Anyway, you'll be grateful one day when I die. They'll be worth thousands.'

I glance at the row of rubbish lining the Spanish arch above her head. Three 'Our Lady of the Rosary', two of Jesus amongst His flock and one of Him on the cross, and several Elvis in Vegas. 'Don't die yet, will you, Mam?' I grin.

What's left of her over-plucked eyebrows nearly shoot into orbit. 'What do you mean, love? Of course I won't!'

I roll my eyes at her then she laughs. 'You and your jokes, I don't know.'

Dad enters then. He is wearing a sharp suit, white shirt, cool tie, as he always does for work. Riddick ought to have consulted Tony-boy when he decided to bring back a proper dress code.

* * *

I drink my tea, staring out of the kitchen window, waiting to catch a glimpse of Mackiness. She'd been leaving earlier and earlier all week, getting the bus three stops on. Avoiding me. Avoiding all of us. She was such a snob but I'd give anything to go out with her. Some might say—but they'd have to be rock hard and carrying a sawn-off to say it—that I was out of Erin's league, just like Chantal's out of mine. But what can you do? A guy likes a challenge.

And there she goes now. Look at that blonde hair— it's fantastic. She is *so* hot! Chantal looks like a washed-out rag next to her. I get up, swilling the remains of my tea down the sink, grabbing my bag. Today, Mackiness, before the weekend begins, you will talk to me, despite that manky look on your face. 'See you later,' I mumble, dashing out before Mum can land one of her sloppy smackers on me.

'What time will you be home?' she calls after me.

'The usual,' I tell her. 'No—later—got soccer practice.'

Mum nods, then pulls a letter from beneath the chipped Diana. 'Oh, give this to Thomas—it's from his mum. Tell him I asked after her and the kids, bless them.'

She hands me the crumpled white envelope and I stuff it into my back pocket.

'Yeah, yeah,' I say, anxious to go. Erin will be halfway down Newstead Road by now, if I don't watch it.

'Have you got your key?' Mum says, as she always does, following me to the door and whispering, 'If I'm not in when you get home it's because I'll be sorting out the disco for you-know-what.'

You-know-what. Dad's fortieth. His big surprise party that he's known about for months. Mum doesn't know that he knows but we've all got to keep quiet to keep her happy. 'OK.'

'Be careful crossing that road.'

Typical. I've got one of them worried I can't cross a road properly and the other worried I'm going to make him a grandad. I wish they'd make their minds up.

'Yeah, see you.'

Mam gives me her my-adored-son look. 'Have a nice day, precious.'

I will have a nice day if I can get Mackiness to talk to me properly. I hurry after her, not too fast to make it look obvious. She's already passed the bus stop she should wait at but it's way too early for Chan or any of that lot to hassle me about why I'm not waiting there either. I continue, until I reach the precinct on Four Lanes End. I have almost caught up with her when she stops abruptly outside Quarashi's shop and I have to say something or it'll look weird. 'Morning,' I greet her.

She spins round, sees it's me and pulls a face. What is it with her? I go alongside, wondering what to say. She makes me nervous. I'm never nervous with bints but she makes me nervous. 'Are you following me?' she asks, straight out.

'Course not. I'm power-walking.' Power-walking? Where had that come from?

'Don't let me stop you,' she says.

'What?'

'Power-walking—I've got to call in here.'

'Oh, right, yeah, see you later.'

'Bye.' I have no choice but to power-walk on and wait at the next bus stop. There's no one here I know—just a few wimpoid Year Eights and a pair of drongoes from Year Eleven. I'm debating whether to have a fag or not—I'm trying to cut down—when Erin arrives.

She stands right next to me, casually dropping her bag onto the pavement, and begins to read a magazine. I glance at the captions. 'My battle with bulimia/I was stalked—by my teacher/I lap-danced for pocket money—a thirteen year old tells all.' She's paid two pounds fifty for that depressing stuff? I hope she's not that wasteful with money when we're married.

And I'm still stood there, not able to think of a chuffing word to say, when the geeks next to her start pratting around, shoving and pushing into each other until they knock Erin sideways into me. I automatically reach out to steady her but let go instantly in case she thinks I'm trying it on, but she keeps her hand on my arm for ages and I am on fire. I can feel my head burning. I feel sick and dizzy and stupid. 'Thanks—sorry,' she says, eventually letting go.

I manage to mumble something cretinous like, 'I won't charge you this time', when the bus arrives and she's gone, following the Year Eleven drongs downstairs. There's no room—I'd have to stand and obviously I never stand. I traipse upstairs, joining the gang, fending off questions about where I've been. I can't talk. I'm in love.

Tommo looks knackered. He plonks himself down next to me in registration. 'What's up with you?' I ask, slipping him his letter.

He glances at it, smiles to himself, then slides it into his shirt pocket for later. 'Nothing but the sky, my friend, nothing but the sky.'

'Thought you were calling round last night?'

He shrugged, scratched his head, shrugged again. 'Couldn't get out,' he mumbles, 'you know what it's like.'

I nod. I knew just what it was like at Tommo's house. Alky father, right as rain one minute, mental the next. Getting worse and worse since Tommo's mam bunked off to Scotland, taking the other kids with her. That's who the letter's from—his mam. She sends stuff to our house because she doesn't want Benny to know where she lives. I don't blame her, I just wish she'd chosen somewhere nearer so Tommo could see her more often. I know he misses her and the sprogs like mad but he stayed behind. Mam says it's because they won't take lads over thirteen at the refuge but I think it's because he didn't want to leave—didn't want to leave the team, didn't want to leave me, didn't want to leave Benny alone.

I want Tommo to come and live at our house. We've got plenty of space since Dad bought next door—plenty, but Tommo won't. Too loyal, like.

Tommo whacks his bag on to the desk and uses it as a pillow. 'Wake me up when Midge comes in,' he says.

'OK,' I tell him. I notice the beginning of a bruise just below his cheekbone. That's loyalty for you.

I glance round the form room, looking for Erin. She's sitting in the corner with Hannah and Owens and that Katia. Weird choice of mates, if you ask me. That Hannah's always so serious; one of those Greenpeace types. Katia fancies me like mad—it is so obvious, man, but there's no way. She's fat for a start—must be knocking on for a size twelve at least. No, no way— rather have Chantal than that. As for Owens—what does she see in him? He's such a wimp. You should see him on the soccer pitch, man—he always looks as if he's going to wet himself when the ball comes any- where near him. Mackiness stands out from the lot of them by a mile. A long, hot mile.

I wish Midge, our form tutor, would hurry up so I could get to French. Best thing we ever did, getting kicked out of Crecy's. Three hours a week sitting behind Erin. There is a God, He is a man, and He sup- ports Man United.

On that thought, Mr Midgley, ex-Leicester City reserves (ha-ha!) walks in. Late, naturally. He's a good bloke is Midge—he's head of Sports Studies. Sports Studies and art are the only decent subjects there are at Adams. I nudge Tommo awake and sit back, waiting for my name to be called, good as gold. Midge flicks through the register dead quick, tells us to line up for assembly and asks for Tommo and me to stay behind. 'You're coming to practice tonight, aren't you?' he asks.

'Course.'

'Good. I want you both spot-on for next week— we've got Glaisdale in the semi-finals and . . . ' he pauses, scowls at Tommo. 'That's *if* you can get your acts together and take things seriously for once. Are you hung over, Boyle?'

'No, sir,' Tommo replies.

'Pull the other one, lad.'

'We'll be there tonight, sir, no problemo,' I say.

Midge glances at me, back to Tommo. He frowns. I know he's seen the bruise but he doesn't say anything. Midge knows the score with Benny—he's dropped us off home after matches enough times—but he knows when to leave things and when to push. Today he left it; stalking off down the corridor to blast out some noisy latecomers.

I let assembly and maths wash over me and then it's on to French. Blackhead's away so we have this supply teacher, Mrs Castle she says her name is. Never seen her before; typical teacher—navy blue cardi,

M&S blouse, dodgy haircut, starts off trying to be hard.

The new bint starts reading instructions at us from this sheet of paper. I'm hardly listening; too busy watching Erin taking down the details. I love the way her hair fans out across her back as she leans forward but it's the colour of it that gets me—a sort of light gold; no—the colour of pinewood before it's been treated. I sigh heavily. Katia twists round, smiles, then twists back. Bog off, Katia—I don't want you.

Tommo's miles away, scratching something into his pencil tin with his compasses.

A worksheet lands on my desk. I glance at it, then tell this Castle person I can't do it.

'Nonsense,' she snaps, 'you're top set.'

'We're not,' I tell her, pointing to Tommo and me. 'Blackhead—Mr Whitehead—sets us separate work to do.'

She glares at me. 'Well, you'll just have to do the same as everyone else today. I haven't been given any alternative instructions.'

'We can't do it.'

'Try,' she says and walks off.

I try. I don't want to look thick in front of Erin but I can't understand a bloody word. I hate French anyway—what a waste of time—and I am super-crap at it. 'Can you do this?' I ask Tommo.

Tommo might be in all the dosser sets with me but he's smart enough when he wants to be. Today's not the day, though. He shakes his head without even looking at the sheet, still scratching away with his compasses on his pencil tin. I raise my hand. Dead polite, playing by the rules. 'I can't do this sheet, Mrs Castle. Can Erin help me?' You genius, Droy, I think to myself.

This Mrs Castle is standing at the front, giving me a dead-eye. 'No, I don't want any talking, just get on with it. You must be able to do the first three questions at least.'

I decide Mrs Castle is a stupid bitch but I don't want any trouble so I get on with something else. See, I'm acting sensibly, using my initiative, doing my graphics products homework. I'm quite happy, sitting behind Erin, inventing a new logo, being creative. I'm good at drawing, see, like I said, and sports. Let me draw or play soccer all day and I'd be top of the school.

After a couple of minutes, the Castle woman comes up to us. 'Why aren't you working?' she asks Tommo. He doesn't bother answering. 'And you!' she says, glaring down at me. 'What do you think you're doing? That isn't French!'

A glob of spit lands on my sheet, just missing my design. 'Watch it, this is coursework!' I tell her.

'It's not what you were supposed to be doing,' she says in a forced whisper. 'If you don't do as you're told your name will go on the board.'

She's beginning to bore me now. 'Not that! Anything but that,' I tell her in a squeaky voice. Tommo laughs.

She starts giving it some. 'That's enough! You can report to Mr Riddick's office at lunchtime.'

'What for?' I reply.

I can feel the mood in the classroom change. Now nobody is doing their stupid worksheets. She hesitates. This can go one way or another, depending on what she says next. She knows it. I know it. We all know it.

Without warning, there's this thud on Tommo's desk. Mrs Castle bangs her hand down but before she can say whatever crap she was going to say, she lets out this 'kin' massive scream. I look down and there's Tommo's compasses sticking out of the back of her hand. No blood or anything, just these silver compasses, wobbling about. All hell breaks loose and she's yelling, 'Get someone, somebody, get someone, I've been stabbed!'

Next minute daft cow Crecy's stood there, eyes popping out. She's going, 'What 'as 'appened? What 'as 'appened?'

I look at Tommo and Tommo looks at me and we just crack up. Man, it's the funniest thing that's ever ''appened' and we are killing ourselves. Even later, in front of Riddick, we can't stop. We try, we really try, but every time I go to explain, I just keep seeing the compasses wobbling about and crack up again.

We get suspended, of course.

6

Neither of us has ever been suspended before. We're not yobs, Tommo and me. We muck around, sure, and we've had our fair share of detentions but we're not the worst kids in the school, not by a long chalk. From the way Riddick bangs on about 'the incident' you'd think we'd been tooled up and taken out half the year group like they do in America.

After the grilling, we're dumped in reception, to have a 'think' about our actions and to wait until our parents can be contacted to pick us up. Castle's already disappeared and apparently we'll be lucky if she doesn't press charges. Talk about overreacting.

It's quiet in reception. Everyone's in period two, bar us. It feels weird, especially as I'm forced to stare at one of my pieces of art work from Year Nine. Skill it is—a pair of muddy football boots in chalk and charcoal. They want to take it down before it curls at the edges, lazy gits.

Tommo's looking down at the carpet, tapping his feet. I guess that he's nervous about his dad arriving, in case he's blathered. 'Come home with me,' I tell him, 'Mam won't mind. You know what she's like.'

'Nah.'

'Go on, we can play pool—the table's set up properly next door now—it'll be a doss.'

'Nah, I'll give it a miss, get some kip. I'll see you at the Centre tomorrow night.'

'Why not tonight?'

He shrugs. 'I'm saving up.'

'What for, your birthday?'

'No, to get to Scotland.'

This is news to me but I don't show it. 'Oh, right.'

'It's about fifty quid on the coach.'

'It will be.'

He knows all he has to do is ask and I'd give him his fare but he's got this proud streak has Tommo. He'd rather slog up and down the estate in all weathers delivering newspapers for a few lousy quid a week. Weird.

'How'd you get the bruise?' I ask.

'Mucking about.'

'Yeah, right.'

Tommo looks up, grins. 'No, really. Dad was in a great mood last night. He's OK now if I drink with him—it keeps him company, slows him down. We were having this really good talk about when he was on the picket lines during miners' strike and how the police tried to arrest him. He elbowed me in the face but it was an accident. Straight up.'

'If you say so, mate.'

'Midge won't be pleased; we'll miss the Glaisdale match,' Tommo states.

I groan. 'He'll kill us.'

There's a long pause. Something else dawns on me now that I've got my head together. Erin. The look on her face as I'd passed her on the way out. Well disgusted. I'd blown it big time. 'Erin's going to think I'm a right prick,' I mutter.

'Erin? So what?' Tommo asks.

'I fancy her,' I say.

He shrugs. 'What about Chan?'

'What about her?'

'I thought you were an item.'

'No way! She's relegation material, mate.'

'I don't think she knows that.'

'That's her problem. Anyway, I thought you were in there when I was on holiday.'

He scowls. 'I wouldn't do that to you. I only gave her a love bite because she wanted to make you jealous. She's mad on you, even if you are hideous.'

'That's her look out.'

'Well, let her down easy, mate. She's not got that much going for her at home.'

'Why don't you go out with her then, Sir Lancelot?'

'She doesn't want me, does she? It's got to be a two-way thing or it doesn't work.'

'Exactly.'

He shakes his head at me and mumbles something. 'What?' I ask.

'I don't even know how it happened.'

'What?'

'The compass thing. I was miles away; thinking about

Mum and James and Sarah in that grotty refuge place and next thing I know that woman's screaming blue murder. I can't even remember doing it.'

I try to cheer him up, to cheer myself up. 'It was funny, though, Tommo. I will remember that scene until the day I die.'

We clock each other and grin. I can feel the laughter bubble up inside and I know I'll start again, Erin or no Erin, but Mrs Long, the secretary, sticks her head through the glass partition and says, 'I'm still trying to get hold of your father, Thomas, but your father will be here in ten minutes, Liam.'

That shuts me up. 'Mine?'

She nods. 'I couldn't get hold of your mother so in the circumstances I have contacted your father at work. He didn't sound too pleased either, young man.'

He wouldn't do. With some people it was hospitals and dentists. With Tony Droy it was schools. He hates them. They remind him of when he was a nipper, being shunted from one class to the next as his mam and dad moved from one travellers' site to another. And as for teachers—you don't want to get him started. He says he only had one decent teacher ever, a bloke called Sanders who taught woodwork. Sanders was the reason Dad took up carpentry and became interested in furniture but the rest can go hang as far as he's concerned. He's never set foot in Adams High, as far as I know. Mam's the one who does all the parents' evenings and that malarkey.

'This should be interesting,' says Tommo, who knows about Dad's aversion.

* * *

Five minutes later Dad drives up, parks right outside the front entrance, storms in. 'Right,' he says, crooking a finger at me, 'come on,' and heads out again.

Mrs Long calls him back. 'Excuse me, Mr Droy, but I think Mr Riddick would like a word before you go.'

Dad scowls, looks at his watch. 'I'm sorry but I have left a meeting to come here. My wife can talk to Mr Riddick when she gets home.'

But Big-Lugs Riddick's out of his office like a shot, that false smile they save for parents fixed on his face. 'I won't keep you any longer than I have to, Mr Droy, but you will appreciate the gravity of the situation. Please come through.'

Dad shrugs, dragging me with him. 'I'd rather Liam waited outside, Mr Droy,' Riddick says.

'If it's about Liam, he needs to know the score,' Dad replies flatly.

Riddick looks surprised but doesn't say anything. I can tell he's thrown out by my dad. He'll have been expecting some loser with crap clothes, fagging it, not the sharp geezer in the Paul Smith suit so easily out-shining him. Dad sits down and listens to the tale. I bow my head because I know when Riddick uses the word 'compasses' I'll crack up again, so I try to concentrate and think about why I should care and I think about Mr Midgley and I think about Erin and what a prat she must think I am and that helps no end.

'So Liam didn't actually attack Mrs Castle?' Dad

asks, sounding like one of those barrister dudes on TV.

'No,' Mr Riddick agrees, 'but he was instrumental in starting the fracas. Like a small minority of others in this school, your son thinks he can set his own agenda and it won't do. I'm trying to raise standards here.'

Fracas? What's one of them when it's at home?

'What *exactly* did Liam do?' Dad pursues. He's looking Riddick straight in the eye.

Riddick looks uncomfortable and consults this piece of paper in front of him. Dad's got him on the ropes and he knows it. Now that I think about it, I didn't actually do anything, did I? But Riddick manages to read out some cobblers about refusing to work, arrogant attitude, and rudeness to members of staff. 'As you know, Liam's already been moved out of his proper set because of his uncooperative behaviour, Mr Droy,' Riddick finishes. This catches Dad out, mainly because I haven't told him.

'Is that true, Liam?' Dad says, facing me, angry as hell.

Dad knows I will never lie to him. I tell him straight what happened, with both Mme Crecy and Mrs Castle. 'I'm sorry she got stabbed—though it was an accident,' I end. It sounds lame, even to me.

'Well, thank you for your honesty, at least, Liam,' Riddick continues. 'That's exactly what I'm trying to foster here at Adams, but it doesn't change my decision.' He flicks his eyes over me then back to Dad. 'I have suspended both boys for four days, Mr Droy. When he returns on Wednesday, Liam will be expected

51

to fulfil this good behaviour contract, agreed between home and school.' He pulls out a sheet of paper with about a thousand rules on it and hands it to Dad. My heart stops dead for about a second.

I know there's no way Dad can read that sheet, he's what-you-call-it—illiterate. Manages to write his name and that's about it. I know something else, as well; there's no way he'll want Riddick to know he can't read that sheet. I hold my breath and wait to see how Dad gets out of this one.

Riddick carries on obliviously, 'If you agree with everything we can sign it now, Mr Droy. It's pretty straightforward and will hopefully help Liam understand the seriousness of the situation. He is very lucky that I haven't expelled him.'

Dad carefully folds the sheet and slips it inside his jacket. 'I'll read this properly later, if you don't mind, Mr Riddick; I'd like to discuss it with my wife first, before any decision is made. Something as important as this needs both of us to look at it.' Good one, Dad. Very smooth.

'Of course,' Riddick agrees.

'And I can assure you Liam will behave when he gets back.' Dad's voice is low and serious as he shoots me a dirty look and Riddick gives me this self-satisfied raising of his dandruffy eyebrows as if to say, *That's you sorted, sonny,* but it's impossible for me to dislike the fat git any more so I just get ready to stand up.

That's when Riddick blows it. If he'd left it, he'd have won, see. I'd have gone home with a right rollocking, but instead, the idiot leans forward and says, 'I'm sure I don't have to tell you how important a good education is, Mr Droy. Liam's grades are, at best, average, and he struggles to achieve that sometimes.'

Dad's face changes instantly and I know if I look, there'll be a pulse beating away in the side of his neck, as there always is when someone ticks him off. Then Riddick digs the hole deeper for himself. 'I'm afraid your son is going to end up nowhere fast if he doesn't get his act together.'

Dad laughs, trying to be pleasant. 'Do you think so? I left school at fourteen with teachers telling me exactly the same but I've done all right and so will he.'

'But you'd agree things are different nowadays, Mr Droy . . . most employers look for some form of qualification these days.'

Dad shoots that one down straight away. 'I don't! All the qualifications in the world don't make someone a good worker. Give me a lad with a positive attitude any day.'

'I think you're missing my point,' Riddick blusters. 'Further education is the norm now—'

'Oh yeah?' Dad interrupts. 'You think I'm going to let him spend three years in some Mickey Mouse college doing a Mickey Mouse degree in pop music? No way, Mr Riddick. Liam's got a job for life and a company car waiting for him, and so's Thomas, the day they leave here at sixteen. How many of your other Year Elevens can say that? Or even your staff?'

'Well, I'm aware there's no such thing as a job for

life any more . . . ' Riddick begins but Dad's had enough.

'I really must go,' he says, calm-but-firm. Deliberately, he rises to his full height, makes a show of looking at his Rolex before he offers Riddick his hand. Riddick takes it reluctantly and then we're outside, gesturing Tommo to come with us, before Riddick can shut his big gobsmacked mouth.

'Nice one, Dad,' I say to him proudly as we leave the car park, 'you showed him right up.'

Dad turns round to reverse, his face tight, his eyes flicking scornfully over me. 'There was nothing nice about that episode, lad, so you can get that notion straight out of your head.'

I don't get why he's so stressed out so I tell Tommo the good news about the company cars. He laughs and decides on a Mini Cooper. Dad snaps at me, 'Liam, don't go repeating my fairy tales, you plonker. Do I look like an idiot? You'll get a company car when you've earned one, like the rest of my men.'

'But you said . . . '

'What I said in there and what I'm telling you now are two different things, right?'

'Right.'

'And you can start this Saturday. I want you at the workshop, eight thirty sharp.'

'What . . . ?'

'Eight, then.'

''Kin' 'ell, Dad.'

Dad gives me a right mean look. 'And stop all this

"'Kin' 'ell" rubbish! If you're going to swear, swear properly, otherwise keep a civil tongue in your head.'

"'Kin' 'ell, Dad!'

'And you can both turn in next week, as well. Nine till three thirty—school hours. I'm not having you wandering round the town centre getting into trouble. That's what he expects from the likes of us.'

'Will we be earning the minimum wage for our labours, Mr Droy?' Tommo asks politely as he makes a paper plane out of his home-school contract.

'Oh, yes, Thomas, I can guarantee you'll be earning the minimum wage of bugger all,' Dad agrees.

I just don't get people sometimes.

7
ERIN

Mr Riddick would definitely be getting a Christmas card from me this year. Rumour had it, he had suspended Liam and Thomas for four whole days, which meant I could walk back from the bus stop in peace for four whole days.

What morons they were. Killing themselves laughing like that after they'd assaulted that teacher. New supply teachers never get an easy ride, even with top sets, but what happened to Mrs Castle was totally out of order.

As I turned into The Close, I glanced across the patch of grass to the Palais de Droy and hoped Liam would have been grounded for life, though I bet there would be little chance of that. He was bound to have the sort of parents who couldn't care less, which is why he is the way he is in the first place. Morons. In their moronic house with their moronic gnomes.

Still, who was I to criticize? Maybe they didn't know any different. At least the Droys could afford to send their son on a field trip *and* pay for it up front. Even they hadn't stooped so low as to steal their kids' savings. The fact that mine had was like a fresh wound, still too sore to touch. No more had been said, but then seeing as we weren't speaking, that was hardly surprising, was it? I swung open the gate and steeled myself for another evening of Ignore your Family.

Mum was sitting at the table, surrounded by battered shoe boxes full of old photographs and stacks of photo albums. 'Hi,' I said shortly, skirting round the table with the intention of heading straight upstairs.

'Hi,' Mum replied, not looking up. The briefer the conversation, the more points you scored in our version of the game. Since telling them I hated them, we have managed on hello, goodbye, bring your dirty clothes down, goodnight.

As I edged past, Mum suddenly brandished a photograph of me when I was seven, minus both front teeth. 'Look at that! Weren't you sweet?'

I grunted a 'hmph'. It wasn't fair, though. I love looking through old photographs. Resolutely, I dropped the picture onto the table and kept edging but the opposition had another one ready. Me again, holding the new-born Nina awkwardly in my arms.

'You were the only one who could get her to sleep, do you remember?'

'Yes. She was a right pain.' Steady now, Erin, whole sentences will cost you.

'She was colicky,' Mum protested amiably, 'you all were.'

'I wasn't. I was perfect.'

Mum nodded. 'Of course you were. I'd forgotten.

Put the kettle on before you go upstairs, will you, pet? I haven't had a chance all day.' Aha! Delaying tactics. The game was taking a new turn.

I sighed, extremely heavily, but did as I was told. Another Kodak moment was thrust in my direction. 'Look! Caught red-handed, you little minx!'

I couldn't help grinning at the picture. It showed me peering guiltily from under the table one Christmas Eve. By my knees, you could just make out the pile of presents I'd taken from beneath the tree, planning to have just a teeny-weeny peep before putting them back. Unfortunately Dad had spotted me and snapped me coming out for the last one. I smiled, but inwardly only, and handed it back to Mum. 'How was school?' she asked casually.

'OK,' I replied, equally as casually. It was obvious what she was doing. Ensnaring me with photographs so I'd talk to her again. I glanced at her. She glanced back, the shadows under her eyes daring me to stay mad at her. I felt my resolve crumble. Sad eyes, old photographs. No, I could resist this. Four days is not long enough to forgive the loss of an entire inheritance. Still, a few minutes browsing wouldn't hurt. The kettle clicked off the boil. I whisked the milk into the instant coffee so it frothed for a second before turning a murky brown. Council house cappuccino for the lady. I passed her the cup and sat down nearby.

'What are you doing with all these out, anyway?' I asked, despite myself, as she began shuffling the photographs back into the boxes.

'I've been looking for a decent one of me to send to the agency.'

'Agency?'

'A recruitment agency. They're trying to find me something part-time.'

'Oh. I didn't even know you were looking for a job.'

'Well, you haven't been exactly receptive to news recently,' Mum replied, trying to smile, but it didn't quite work; her mouth was set too firmly, her eyes sparkled just that bit too brightly.

'What sort of job?' I asked, ignoring the reference.

Mum shrugged. 'Oh, anything that fits in with school hours. They said there might be something going at Sally Lee's nearer Christmas.'

'The cake factory?' I asked incredulously.

'Yes, the cake factory. What's wrong with that?'

You wouldn't think to hear Mum talk she had three A levels. She would have had a teaching degree, too, if she hadn't packed the course in halfway through to be with Dad. He was two years older and she couldn't bear it when he left college in Brighton to teach miles away in Wolverhampton. That's love for you.

Mum began shuffling stacks of photographs into neat, small piles. 'I've been trying to think of a way to pay for this trip, Erin,' she said quietly. 'What I thought was . . . '

Whatever she thought was interrupted by Georgia and Nina hurtling through the door, screaming and bawling their eyes out. 'What's wrong? What's the matter?' Mum asked, scraping her chair back in alarm.

'Look! Look!' Georgia yelled, holding something in her hand. 'It went into Nina in the garden. It went into her!'

'Throw it down now!' I shouted, when I realized what it was. 'Throw it down now!'

Instantly, she dropped the mud-crusted syringe onto the table, where it landed with a sinister thud.

Nina was crying and shaking her hand. 'It went down my nail, it went down my nail.'

'Let me have a look; let me see,' Mum yelled but Nina shook her head and crossed her arms tightly, closing herself down.

'It hurts,' she sobbed.

'We'd better get her to the doctor's,' Mum said, staring at me with frenzied eyes. I knew she was thinking the same thing I was—hepatitis, or worse, Aids.

'Which doctor's?' I said. 'The old one or have we got a new one?'

'I don't know,' Mum cried, chewing her lip. Her eyes roamed the kitchen for a telephone we didn't have. 'I meant to register at the surgery today but I never got round to it. Should I take her straight to the hospital instead? Oh, I can't. Your father's got the car!'

Nina, catching the rising panic in Mum's voice, began to cry louder. Mum cradled her and Georgia, also crying now, clung primitively to Mum's back. I knew there wasn't time to get hold of Dad, so I dashed out to find help. 'I'll be back in a minute,' I yelled over my shoulder.

* * *

Liam answered the door, his eyes nearly popping out of his head at the sight of me. 'Hiya,' he greeted me. 'What's up?'

'Can I use your phone?' I asked brusquely.

'Who is it, Liam?' a woman's voice asked from somewhere inside.

'It's OK, Mam, it's for me,' he yelled back.

'No,' I said. 'Can your mum drive? My sister's been hurt—we need to get her to the hospital.'

Liam hesitated for a second, then swung the door open to allow me in. I was vaguely aware of a dark hallway covered in ceramic plates and the clammy scent of pot pourri before a petite woman wearing the most figure-hugging top arrived. 'Can I help you, flower?' Mrs Droy asked, flicking over me with blue-tinted eyelashes. I quickly explained what had happened. 'Never!' she exclaimed. 'That's terrible! We'd best get her to St Luke's. That young doctor down here wouldn't have a clue.' She grabbed her car keys immediately and trotted out.

We all piled into the back of the Droy's roomy car leaving Liam sitting at the front with his mother. 'Lucky the hospital's off the main roads; I can't do motorways or anything like that, I have panic attacks, you know,' Mrs Droy informed us, not exactly filling me with confidence. She rabbited on about what a shame Nina's injury was and how the neighbourhood had changed since they'd moved there when Liam was a baby and how she'd wanted to buy somewhere in the country but Liam's dad, who was called Tony and owned all the Pine Island shops, by the way, didn't see why we should move when we'd put all that work into the house so when next door's came up they bought that and knocked through, though you wouldn't believe it but there's still not room for everything.

She reminded me of those telesales people who try to deliver their pitch in one huge sentence so you can't say 'no' before they've finished. Even Nina calmed down, her sobs gradually decreasing until they seemed to settle for soft hiccups, serenading Mrs Droy's breathless monologue. All I could think of to do was to stroke Nina's rigid legs, hoping it would help.

Eventually we squealed into St Luke's car park and drew up between two ambulances. 'Do you want us to wait for you, love?' Mrs Droy asked Mum. 'You can be hours in these places.'

'No—thanks—I'll call my husband at work to pick us up once I've sorted everything out. If you know the way to reception, that would help,' Mum replied, sliding awkwardly out of the car with Nina in her arms.

Mrs Droy twirled round and nodded, her blonde fringe flopping over her eyes. 'Course I do. I know this place like the back of my hand. Spent enough time in here with you as a toddler, didn't I, Liam?' She turned and mouthed 'undescended testicle' at me.

Liam told her to shut up and almost bolted out of the car but I was too distressed myself to take advantage of his distress. 'Will Nina be all right?' Georgia whispered to me as I grabbed her hand and followed Mum through the automatic doors of the main entrance.

'I don't know,' I replied honestly. I glanced round. It was bizarre, being here, for this reason. People like us fell off ponies or broke our legs on skiing holidays. We didn't get stabbed by infected needles. That was for the Scrunchies.

Liam hung back, waiting for me as his mum and mine talked urgently to the receptionist. He offered Georgia some gum, which she took with a shy smile. 'The Walesbys weren't smackheads or anything, you know, in case you were wondering,' he said, offering me a piece. I declined. I was grateful for the lift but I wanted him to go now. I didn't want him here, Mr Smooth Operator, with his footballer's tan and designer clothes, witnessing our trauma.

'Yeah, right,' I muttered.

'I think one of them had that thing where you have fits—you know, if you don't eat biscuits.'

'Diabetes?'

'Yeah, that's it—diabetes. They have to inject themselves, don't they? Maybe it was one of those needles.'

'Yeah, well, you'd know,' I snapped.

He looked puzzled. 'What do you mean?'

'Anything to do with injecting people.'

'I don't do drugs—drugs are for losers!' he said vehemently.

'I meant Mrs Castle,' I replied coolly.

Liam was fuming. ''Kin' 'ell, Mackiness, that wasn't even me!'

63

'It might as well have been!'

'Get real.'

'You get real.'

He turned to Georgia, who had been listening with great interest. 'Is she always so up herself?' he asked her.

She smirked. 'Yes, all the time.'

Fortunately, before the traitor had a chance to relate further lies about me, Mum waved me across. She was being directed by a nurse down a side wing. I nudged Georgia forward, passing Mrs Droy on the way. 'Let me know how you get on, won't you, flower?' she asked. She looked genuinely concerned so I nodded. After all, it wasn't her fault her son was a jerk with undescended testicles.

The next couple of hours were horrible. Georgia and I had to wait outside the drawn curtains as the doctors examined Nina but we could hear everything. Then Mum came out, looking whiter than the nurse's apron, and whispered that they were going to have to take Nina's whole nail off as a precaution, before returning to Nina. I felt instantly sick and knew Georgia did too, so we trundled off back to reception to wait for Dad.

It was all over by the time he arrived and a calmer Nina was brandishing her bandaged forefinger like a trophy. 'I bet I'll have to show everyone in Special Assembly,' she beamed.

'Did they have to take the whole nail off? That's a bit drastic, isn't it?' Dad asked, carefully scooping Nina up in his arms as we headed for the car park.

'They have to treat all needle-stick injuries seriously,

in case,' Mum replied. Her voice sounded far away, almost trance-like.

'In case of—oh, I see,' Dad said, his voice croaky. He drew Nina closer to him, patting her back gently as he walked.

'We'll know more when they let us know the results of the blood tests,' Mum whispered as she strode alongside them.

'Well, I don't know what the world's coming to sometimes,' Dad replied sadly as he lowered Nina to the ground so he could unlock the car door.

'I'm going to draw a face on my bandage when I get home,' Nina announced.

'No you're not! You must keep it clean!' Mum snapped. Her cheeks flushed instantly as she realized how mean she sounded. 'Well, she must! The nurse said,' she added defensively, helping Nina into the Espace and buckling her up.

We drove home in silence.

8

Out of all of us, Nina seemed the least upset by what had happened but that was probably because she didn't know about the tests and the long wait for the results. 'We're getting a phone because of my finger,' she informed me cheerfully at breakfast the next morning.

'Are we?' I asked, glancing at Mum. She nodded and I felt my heart race. At last, after everything, a hint of normality. I picked Nina up and hugged her tight, chanting, 'We're getting a phone, we're getting a phone.'

'It's for emergencies only,' Dad declared, 'so don't get excited.'

'I know,' I answered, dropping Nina. 'Where will we put it? In the hall?'

'I don't know. Ask your mum.'

'Mum?'

'I don't know, I haven't thought,' she replied flatly.

'You can have it connected in my room; it's always for me anyway,' I bragged.

Mum managed only the remotest of smiles as she briskly wiped the table down with the dishcloth, avoiding the area where Dad was sitting like a car swerving to avoid a pheasant.

'Is anything wrong?' I asked.

'Not at all,' Mum replied but everything about her suggested the opposite.

Dad replied on her behalf. 'Yes there is something wrong, Erin. Believe it or not, your mother's in a mood because I've found a job.'

'A job? That's great, isn't it?' I glanced from one to the other.

'You'd think so, wouldn't you?' Dad muttered from behind the paper.

Mum glowered at the headlines. 'Yes, a job, a professional job like the head of IT going at Glaisdale I showed you, not agreeing to stay on with the council as a "handyman" for three hundred pounds a week!'

'You're overreacting, as usual. It'll be more than that,' Dad snapped but I could tell from his defensive tone it wouldn't be much more.

Mum fired back immediately. 'Overreacting? As usual? Thank you, Noel. It's nice to know you hold my opinions in such high esteem. I just happen to think that if anyone's going to be working for peanuts it should be me, the one without the degree and years of experience, not you!'

'Peanuts? How can you work for peanuts?' Nina giggled but I shot her a warning look. She wasn't old enough to read the danger signs yet. Mum and Dad didn't argue much but when they did they were real humdingers and this one was building up a treat.

67

Georgia, more tuned in, slid from her chair and took Nina with her. 'We'll go get ready,' she said wisely. I, Obi-Wan Kenobi, had taught her well.

'What a good idea,' Dad said over-enthusiastically. 'We'll all get ready to go to town. Hurry up with breakfast, Erin—I don't want to be all day. The rugby's on at two.'

'Em, I've got everyone coming round this afternoon, remember? I want to do my homework before they arrive.'

'Oh, have you? I don't remember being informed,' he mumbled crossly.

'Well, Mum knows.'

I looked at Mum for support. She sighed heavily. 'I'd forgotten. Do you think it's a good time?'

'But it's been arranged for ages,' I said quietly, 'it's too late to cancel now.'

'Well, just don't make a mess,' Mum said as if I was three years old.

Eventually they went and I was left alone. I welcomed the stillness of the house and the temporary freedom of being on my own. At first, Mum and Dad's argument lingered heavily like petrol fumes in the air. It was the first time they had been so openly hostile to each other in months. There had been one huge, plaster-cracking row when Dad first told her about Steve Rawlinson and the bankruptcy but since then it had been all 'Dad needs our support' and 'we must pull together' stuff from Mum. I didn't have time to dwell on it, though. The gang were due in an hour and I hadn't even made my bed.

I dashed upstairs, ignored my homework and spent the hour trying to make my bedroom more appealing but there's only so much foul football wallpaper you can hide with two cushions and a lava lamp and in the end I slumped miserably on top of the duvet and gave up.

Maybe Mum had been right; it wasn't a good time to bring friends round. In fact, there was never going to be a good time. What was I thinking, inviting them to this dump? None of my friends lived on a council estate. OK, OK, I know about true friends not judging you on your possessions and all that stuff but all of mine lived in such great places. Katia lived in a brand new 'executive' detached house on Coney Heights; she had her own bathroom and everything. In fact, her bathroom was larger than my bedroom. Hannah's house was Victorian, like The Lodge, reminding me of what I was missing, and even though Gabriel's place was owned by the church and enshrined in last century's anaglypta, it was better than this. I began to feel frazzled and desperately stuffed all Georgia's Beanie babies into a pillowcase and hid them under the bed to make more space. It would have to do.

The idiotic thing was that within two minutes of their arrival, it was like it always was in The Lodge, easy and noisy and mad. They all had more important things on their minds than my dire decor. Hannah talked about her mum's test results not being back yet and how it was making everyone tense at home. I could identify with that! Gabriel wanted to know which one of us would do his chemistry homework and Katia had seen a 'gorgeous' top in town that she wanted our opinion about. She knew how to put problems in perspective, that girl.

'High Street clothes are such a rip off,' Gabriel told her. 'Take this fine piece of knitwear, for example,' he declared, glancing down at one of his 'grandad' specials, a yellow and sage-green diamonds down the front job with leather buttons like miniature hot cross buns. 'I got this for seventy-five pence in the Age Concern shop. And it's machine washable.'

'Gabriel, it's foul,' Katia said succinctly.

We argued about charity clothes for ten minutes, then I told them about Nina's episode and they all squirmed. 'Stop it! Stop it!' Hannah pleaded, shaking her hands around. 'I hate anything to do with needles.'

We then launched into our various gruesome experiences with injections of the needle coming through the entire arm variety until she pleaded with us to change the subject.

'Right,' Katia agreed, dragging my magazine on to her lap and flicking through the pages. 'Let's see who's been writing to Lydia, our advice expert, this month. Oh, look, Ernie, there's one from you.'

'Yeah, course there is,' I said, rolling my eyes at Hannah.

'Dear Lydia,' Katia began, in a bimbo voice, I've

made a big mistake. I gave a boy I met at a party oral sex and now I've got a sore throat and a stomach ache. Could I be pregnant? And do you think I should tell anyone about this? Robbie fan, Derbyshire. Lydia, your reply, please.'

I, Lydia, chose standard BBC for my voice on this occasion. 'Well, Robbie Fan, the good news is you are not pregnant, the bad news is you are stupid and should get yourself down to the library and find a picture of a woman's anatomy, where you will clearly see the digestive system and the reproductive system are two entirely separate things. Next problem, please.'

'But that doesn't explain the stomach ache, Lydia,' Gabriel interrupted.

'Or the sore throat, Lydia,' Hannah added. 'We teens expect explicit responses to our explicit questions.'

Katia giggled. 'It's supposed to taste horrible.'

'What is?'

'You know, the stuff.'

'What stuff?' Hannah asked innocently.

'Do I have to spell it out? There's a member of the clergy present.'

'Don't mind me,' Gabriel grinned, 'I'm all ears.'

As the penny dropped, so did Hannah's jaw. 'Yuck!' she said, throwing a punch at Katia's arm. 'And how would you know?'

'My mum told me.'

'Your mum!' we chorused.

Katia nodded casually. 'What's wrong with that? We talk about everything.'

'But you must have limits,' I said. 'I can talk to mine about most things but not *that* detailed. And how does she know?'

'She was a punk in the seventies, what more can I say?' Katia replied coolly.

Hannah picked at her nail. 'My mum didn't even tell me about periods. She just left a leaflet on my bed with a packet of Kotex normal flow,' she announced. 'I wouldn't mind but it was two years after I'd started.'

'Same here,' Gabriel joked. Our laughter was joined by muffled snorting from outside and I sprang from the bed to yank open the door. Georgia stood there, not even bothering to look ashamed at being caught ear-wigging. 'Go away,' I told her. We'd made a deal last night. She gets lost when I have friends round, I get lost when she does.

'I'm only delivering a message,' she retorted.

'Deliver it, then.'

'Mum wants you.'

'What, now?'

Georgia glanced behind, then looked at me, her face slightly crumpled. 'They're arguing again. They've been horrible all morning. I don't like it,' she whispered.

I leaned forward, pulling the door to at the same time. 'Ignore them. Parents argue; it's their job.'

'Mum wants you,' she repeated sullenly.

I sighed heavily. 'Back in a mo,' I shouted into my bedroom.

'OK, Gabriel, you're Lydia this time,' Katia announced, 'choose a good one.'

I found Mum alone in the kitchen, her back to me. 'What's up?' I greeted her.

'Can you ask your friends to go home, please, Erin. I've got a headache and I can't do with all the commotion this afternoon,' she replied, not turning round.

Her voice was quiet and wavering but the words hit me like gravel against a window pane. 'What? They've only just got here!'

'Erin, please don't argue, just do it.'

This was so unfair. 'Great! I finally pluck up the courage to invite them over and you kick them out. Thanks a lot.'

'Please, Erin.'

'This is pathetic.'

'Yes, it is,' she agreed.

Nobody asked why. My face was enough to tell them not to. Hannah used her mobile to call her mum and the next half hour waiting for Mrs Brough to pick them up was one of the longest, most humiliating, of my life. We kept talking, but it felt strained and super-ficial, and when they left I would have given anything to join them in that Volvo.

Downstairs, Georgia and Nina were watching a video, the sound barely audible. 'Where's Mum?' I asked sharply.

'Having a lie down,' Georgia responded.

'We've got to be quiet,' Nina added. They both looked subdued.

'And Dad?'

'Clearing the garden,' Nina answered. 'We can play out when he's finished.'

'Right,' I said. I was fed up with this. I was going to get this family sorted once and for all.

Dad wasn't so much clearing as attacking the garden. I watched him as he shovelled and stabbed the long clumps of grass that sprouted haphazardly between rough paving slabs. He worked erratically, starting on one section then being distracted by something further along before going back to where he started. His face had a ruddy glow from all the digging and he looked almost boyish. 'Found any more needles?' I asked, my eyes scanning the dark oblongs of dead grass.

Dad shook his head. 'No, nothing like that.'

'Those Walesbys must have been such dead-beats.'

'Maybe.' Dad took a breath and stared around. 'It's not a bad sized plot this, you know, Erin, it could make a nice garden. Mr Black next door's is fabulous—have you seen his dahlias?'

I admitted I had not. 'I was thinking of growing some vegetables in the corner over there and planting some shrubs down the side of the fencing there . . . ' Dad continued, 'and what about a playhouse at the bottom for the girls to use?'

'We won't be here long enough for all that, will we?' I asked.

Dad hunched his shoulders against the directness of

my question. 'We're going to be here for a while,' he said.

'What do you call a while?'

'Oh, at least a couple of years, I should think.'

I gawped at him. A couple of *what* did he say? Years? Years as in those things that have twelve whole months in one of them? Some mistake surely? I had come out with the intention of asking what was going on with him and Mum but this was much more serious. 'You're joking, right, Dad? You've nearly finished your community service. You can just get a proper job then, can't you, and we'll have money again?'

'Meaning working as a handyman isn't a proper job?'

'You know what I mean!'

'It isn't that simple, Erin.'

'Yes it is.' Course it was.

'No, it isn't. I can't seem to get this through to your mother, either. I'm bankrupt, remember.'

'So?'

Dad sighed, his eyes fixed on the broken fence at the bottom of the garden, where litter gathered like plaque between the crooked planks. I knew from the way he was concentrating on the rubble he was getting irritated with me but I had to make my point. 'It's horrible here, Dad. We don't belong—we don't fit.'

He stopped raking to look at me, his eyes puzzled. 'Fit? Who fits anywhere, Erin? I certainly don't think I'm "fit" to return to the classroom again. Killing myself over targets and long-term planning and league tables. For what? A nervous breakdown by fifty? I think I prefer life on the allotment or working behind a bar somewhere—minimum wage, minimum stress.'

I had never heard him talk like this. The allotment? Working behind a bar? He'd be joyriding next. 'But, Dad, you're the thing . . . you're the breadwinner. We're all relying on you to get us out of here.'

What had been a healthy, boyish glow on Dad's cheeks had turned into a deep, uneven red, like wine spilt across a white tablecloth. 'Then don't,' he replied flatly. And turned away from me.

I stormed to the back door, fighting back angry tears, banging mud off my shoes against the step. Was this it, then? Was this our life from now on? A mother with headaches all the time and a self-centred father growing cabbages between pulling pints? All because of money. Money, money, stupid money. I gave my shoes a final bang but the mud clung stubbornly to the soles. That was all I needed, being yelled at for bringing mud into the house—like it mattered.

I shrugged off my shoes and kicked them into the corner of the step. Money, money, money. It made me sick. No money. No security. Just arguments and tension. Not being able to have friends round in case you made too much noise. What should we do, Georgia, Nina, and me? Go to the Centre and hang out with the Scrunchies? Start legging school and shoplifting? Drugs? We wouldn't have to go far, would we? Just the back garden! Just the back garden where we had crops of the stuff. Not dahlias, Dad, not on our side of the fence.

I couldn't wait to be grown up. I'd move as far away from The Close as I could possibly get and I'd make sure I had a huge house, all paid for, before I even thought about bringing kids into the world. And I would never, ever take out a loan in my life.

Never.

I stomped through into the kitchen with the intention of making myself a cup of tea and stuffing my face with biscuits but the sight of Mrs Droy, sitting upright at the table, jigging Nina up and down on her knee, caught me by surprise. 'Hello, love,' she smiled. 'I was just passing and thought I'd pop by to see how the little girl was. And she's just dandy, aren't you, treasure?'

'Treasure' was double dandy judging by the enormous carton of Celebrations clasped to her chest.

'I invited Mrs Droy in to wait,' Georgia explained pompously. 'I didn't want to seem rude.'

Mrs Droy, easily fooled, made some comment about middle one's lovely manners. 'Er . . . Mum's upstairs and Dad's gardening,' I said. 'Shall I get them?'

'Dad's only doing the garden because they've had a big row. He wants to watch the rugby, really,' Nina informed us.

'Shush, Nina,' I said.

Mrs Droy laughed and winked at me. 'Don't worry, love, we do a lot of "gardening" in our house, too.'

I decided Mrs Droy was all right. Liam obviously took after his father.

Carefully, Mrs Droy began to prise herself away from Nina's chocolatey presence and said she had to be off, but Mum entered just as she was preparing to leave. Mum's hair was flattened to one side where she had been resting and her face had that half-awake, half-asleep look. Hastily, she re-set her features from 'not-quite-with-it' to 'oh, lovely, we've got a guest', in that speedy way adults have. 'Would you like a cup of tea?' Mum asked automatically. Offer readily accepted.

'This is a table and a half,' Liam's mum commented as Mum filled the kettle. She ran both hands appreciatively along the grain. I noticed every finger had at least one jewel-encrusted ring attached to it.

'Oh, yes,' Mum agreed vaguely. 'I thought the removal men were going to have to saw it in two to get it through the door when we moved in.'

'It's beautiful,' Mrs Droy continued.

Mum beamed. 'It's been in the family for years. It came from my grandparents' farmhouse in the Dales originally.'

Nina added her bit. 'You mustn't spill Ribena on it or draw smiley faces in felt pen,' she told a laughing Mrs Droy.

'I won't, ducky, I promise. My Tony would love this—I told you he's in pine, didn't I?'

Mum cast a wary eye over Nina and said she couldn't remember because everything about yesterday was still a blur. There was a quick recap on My Tony, his career in carpentry so far. I excused myself, using the homework clause. Mrs Droy clasped her hands together, which must have hurt. 'What I would give to hear our Liam say that!' she exclaimed.

Dream on, missis.

My mother, used to my diligent nature and therefore less easily impressed, said fine, I could go, before adding, 'We need to have a talk later, Erin.'

Funny that. We were always needing to 'have a talk'. Never got round to one though, did we?

This occasion was no exception. Mrs Droy stayed for hours, so by the time dinner was over and Nina had been given a bath and other displacement activities both Mum and Dad were beyond *the talk*. Instead, in the time honoured tradition of Mackiness Slanging Matches, we left it to fester and watched *Lifeswaps* instead.

On Monday, I dreaded having to tell Mr Whitehead about the trip but he was away again. Once more, those with cheques for the deposit were told to bring them 'next time'. I tutted at the inconvenience along with the rest of them, shameless being that I was.

At home, an uneasy truce had descended. Mum and Dad were back on shrugging terms so by Tuesday I felt brave enough to invite Katia back to do some coursework. She was ecstatic about coming home on the bus with me until I reminded her Liam was still suspended so she wouldn't see him.

'I might,' she said, undeterred, 'if we stroll past his house enough times.'

'That's right,' I said, 'because being too obvious and desperate always works with the opposite sex.'

'Exactly,' she laughed.

It turned out to be Katia's lucky day. Not only did she see Liam but she saw him outside my house. Outside my house loading our kitchen table into the back of a huge Pine Island van. 'What's going on?' I asked, noticing Thomas Boyle was there too, gamely holding on to one corner of the table. Liam, hot and flustered, glanced at me but was concentrating on instructions being fired at him from inside the van. 'Be careful, Liam!' the voice urged. 'Lift it higher.' I left Katia drooling on the pavement.

In the kitchen, Mum was staring blankly at the floor but her dazed expression snapped-to as I asked her what was happening. 'I've sold the table, so you can go to France!' she replied simply.

I should have been happy, but I wasn't. I felt sick. 'But, Mum, it's our best thing!'

She put her arms round my shoulders and kissed me on the cheek. 'It's only a table. I was going to tell you on Friday but with one thing and another . . . then when I got talking to Bonita . . . '

'Bonita?'

'Mrs Droy—Liam's mum. Do you remember her admiring it? I mentioned I was going to sell it and she said Tony would give me the best price for it and she was right—I had no idea it was worth so much. I've even got enough left over to buy Georgia and Nina some new shoes, so we've done really well.'

'Does Dad know?' I asked. My voice seemed to echo round the room.

She smiled wearily. 'Of course, Dad knows. He thought it was a great idea. It makes him—us—feel better about using the . . . ' She stopped mid-sentence, glancing at the open doorway. '. . . well, you know.'

The savings. Yes, I knew. Somehow, I wasn't as bothered about losing the savings as I was about losing the table. The savings had never been real; just a figure written down in a passbook. I'd been mad, sure, but more about them not telling me than them actually spending it. But the table. 'But the table . . . ' I said, repeating my thoughts out loud, staring at what now seemed like a vast ocean of space on the floor.

'Is just that, a table, a piece of furniture,' Mum declared, trying to keep her voice level. Who did she think she was kidding? Just a piece of furniture? Only our family history, more like. Only the last decent thing we had from The Lodge, sold to send me on a stupid trip. What is it they say? Be careful what you wish for?

It was even worse when Mr Droy delivered the new one just after Katia had left. Admittedly, it did fit better size-wise but it was a spindly, blanched reproduction that wouldn't last two minutes. I hated it. I wanted our old one back. I wanted to hide under it and snag my tights on it and not spill Ribena across it. I wanted it back.

'It's tacky,' I informed Mum. I was on the point of tears and she knew it.

'It won't always be like this, I promise,' she said, her eyes as damp as mine.

'According to Dad it will,' I mumbled, remembering our conversation at the weekend.

I thought she'd nod in agreement but she didn't. 'Your dad and I have had a long talk, Erin, and he's right, you know. We got caught up in that whole lifestyle deal where he was working all the hours God sends and for what? A bigger car? A ridiculous mortgage we'd never pay off? We never saw him, even at weekends. And the phone never stopped ringing even when he did come home, did it? It was no life, for either of us. I think this whole thing was a blessing in disguise, ridiculous as it seems at this moment. In America they call it down-sizing. Everyone's doing it.'

'I'll bet.'

'Well, one thing I do know is that he's desperately sorry about using your savings.'

'I know. I don't care about that . . . I just . . . ' I sighed, unable to complete the sentence. Everything was changing too fast.

Droy-boy nearly fainted when he realized I was waiting for him the next morning. 'Do you mind if I walk with you?' I asked.

'Sure, I talk to anyone, me,' he said flippantly as I fell into step with him. A deep pink flush stole along the collar of his shirt. I'd noticed it before when he talked to me but I tried not to think of the implications, especially today, with business on the agenda. 'Enjoy your skive?' I asked.

'What, suspension? Some skive. Dad had me working like a navvy.'

I smiled broadly, pleased to have arrived at the main subject so quickly. 'What did you have to do?' I asked casually.

'Shift furniture mainly.'

'Like our table?' I said, trying to laugh, trying to keep it light.

'Yeah. Hernia job that thing.'

'I'll bet. Where did you take it?'

He named one of the Pine Island branches. It made sense. 'Oh,' I said simply. He babbled on, but I was only half listening, planning my next move.

After school I walked into town and headed for London Road. At first, it's pretty seedy, with a few run-down bed and breakfast places interspersed with junk shops and greasy cafés but then the road widens and transforms. The greasy cafés are replaced by smart bistros and trendy restaurants, the junk shops by high class antiques emporia. If I continued for a few hundred more metres, I would reach Hannah's house. If I had continued even further, and crossed over at the park gates, I'd have reached The Lodge. Instead, I stood outside Pine Island and stared into the window at our table.

That night, I wrote a long letter to Liam's father. I knew if I saw him face to face, the words would come out wrong and I'd sound childish. Instead, I composed what I thought was a well crafted plea for him not to sell the table until I could buy it back from him. I pulled out all the emotional stops about it being in the family for years and how not only I used to play under it, but Mum too when she was little. Telling him just how special and important it was to us; how to have it back would give us something to aim for again, like a symbol of a brighter future.

I addressed it to Pine Island on London Road and marked it strictly personal and, just in case the postal service went into liquidation or something, I delivered it by hand. Mr Droy would have to have a heart of stone not to save our table for me.

10
LIAM

'Em . . . unaccustomed as I am to public speaking,' Dad begins, the piece of paper in his hand shaking slightly, either from nerves or drink or both, 'I just want to say how great it is to see you all here tonight—except you, Patrick, you lazy bugger!'

There's uproar as Uncle Patrick, Dad's eldest brother, takes a bow, sloshing beer all down his best suit at the same time. The joke is Uncle Pat, a market trader, has never missed a day's work since he started at fourteen. Tommo doesn't know that but he's still laughing his head off. He's well gone, even though it's not even midnight yet. Still, it's his birthday too. If a geezer can't get canned on his fifteenth, when can he? I've had a couple but I'm not bothering trying to keep up with him—I've got a match tomorrow and want to be focused, not puking half the night.

I look round the marquee. It's jam packed with people from all over the place—auctioneers, cabinet makers, lorry drivers. Dad's family from Cork, Mum's from Kilkenny. A lot of the family are travellers and they have been here the whole week, taking up residence on the grass outside in their chrome-sided caravans. The neighbours haven't complained because they're here, too, digging in to the free booze and food Mam's spent the last six months stressing over. The Droys know how to put on a show, so they do.

Mrs Mack's standing near Mam; they're whispering and laughing together as if they've been buddies for years. Funny how things turn out—if it hadn't been for the little Nina injuring herself, which ended up being nothing, as I predicted, Mam would never have got pally with Mrs Mack. Not that it has done me much good with Erin—I still haven't been promoted further than walking with her to the bus stop—though she's a lot more natural with me now. I find her dead easy to talk to but maybe that's because we're usually comparing notes about how our parents show us up.

Erin isn't here yet—she and her dad are taking it in turn to baby sit or something. Instead I clock Chantal and nod. I wouldn't have invited her but Mam said we should have some 'youngsters' to keep the party going and she only lives a few streets away so I thought, why not? I remember the groping session we had behind the Centre on Wednesday and hope she doesn't mess up my chances with Erin by mentioning it. I'll have to get Tommo to distract her, unless Erin doesn't turn up.

Dad's squinting at the sheet of paper again, codding everyone he's reading from it. I know he's spent days memorizing the words; I've heard him. He's thanking Mam and me now, calling for us to join him on the temporary dance floor we've paid an arm and a leg for. We go up. There's a cheesy pose for our adoring public as a dozen flashlights explode and then I see Erin and she just takes my breath away.

She's wearing this black dress that shimmers and clings in all the right places and her hair is different— all combed up and . . . oh, I'm chronic at thinking of the right words. I swallow hard as she heads straight towards us, nodding and clapping with Katia, the gate-crasher. 'Aww! You looked so sweet and embarrassed,' she teases, squeezing my arm before flinging herself round my mam and telling her she looks 'fab'. I've never seen Erin like this, so—I don't know—pumped up.

'I want to talk to you later, Mr Droy,' she says, pretending to frown and pointing her finger at Dad. 'I've got a bone to pick with you!' What she wants a word with Dad for I've no idea—she's never even met him as far as I can remember. She's slurring some of her words, so it's obvious she's been up to more than watching telly with Georgia and Nina over at number fifteen. I glance at Katia, who looks surprisingly OK tonight but is still nothing compared to her girlfriend. She mumbles something about hoping I don't mind her coming but the party coincided with her sleepover at 'Ernie's'. Course it did.

Erin was still bending Dad's ear over something. 'I look forward to it, sweetheart,' he tells her, a slightly puzzled look on his face, then he grabs hold of Mam. 'How about a dance with an old man?' he grins.

'I thought you'd never ask,' Mam grins back, leading him to the middle of the dance floor.

This I cannot watch. Kids having to witness their parents dancing ought to be made illegal. Boobs-ahoy Bonita's already given half the blokes heart attacks with her version of *Riverdance*. 'Fancy a drink?' I say to Erin.

'Lead the way, big boy,' she replies. Now that's what I call a promising start.

Of course, Katia has to come, too, and Tommo and Chantal, but it's OK because everyone's in a great mood. The bar in the marquee is packed out so I divert us all into the kitchen which is quieter but full of spare booze. I point to the dozen bottles of Hooch Mam bought in especially for us 'youngsters' and we shake our heads at the sadness of it all. 'Haven't touched that since I left juniors,' Tommo says, heading for the Jack Daniels.

'Girls, what can I get you?' I ask.

Katia gives me her full attention. 'Vodka and orange, please, landlord.'

'Blondie?'

'Same,' she says, not bothering to get angry at the name for once. She is staring at the Sacred Heart plate. 'It's lovely, that picture,' she says, then pipes up with some rhubarb about how fantastic it would have been to have met Jesus. What sort of thing is that to say?

'You've been hanging around with Gayboy Owens too long,' I tell her, handing her the drink.

Instant wobbler. 'If by *Gayboy* you mean Gabriel, for your information he's not gay, and even if he was, what's

89

it to you? And he doesn't talk about religion unless we instigate it, so stop taking the mess,' she hisses.

I'm not used to birds having a go at me, especially when they use big words, but I take it from Erin. From her, it's music. Not that I let her think she's getting away with bawling me out. 'OK, OK, don't get your Sloggis in a knot, it was just a joke.'

'One in four people are gay, mate,' Tommo chips in.

'Well, it isn't me,' Chantal says, giving me this cocky look. It's her way of reminding me about last week but I'm not letting on I understand. Not with Erin here.

'And it's definitely not me,' Katia adds brightly. I glance briefly at her. What does that mean? She's been all the way with some guy? I wouldn't have thought it but you never know with posh birds.

'I don't know if it's me or not,' Erin says, all smoothness and light again, 'so I've decided to stay a virgin until I find out.'

'Music to a mother's ears,' Mrs Mackiness laughs and Erin nearly dies on the spot. Her face glows and we don't help by killing ourselves laughing.

Mrs Mack laughs too and tells Erin she's going and asks if she's got her key. Erin nods dumbly, thinking if she doesn't talk, her mum won't guess how much she has had to drink. Been there, done that. Luckily, Mrs Mack has a bit of the old wine glow to the cheeks herself so I ask her if she wants me to walk her across The Close. She gives my face a nip and says I'm a lovely boy but she'll manage.

'Don't go tripping over the trailers now,' I tell her as she waves goodbye.

'Do you think she could tell I've been drinking?' Erin asks.

'No,' we lie.

Erin blows a strand of hair from her face and shakes her head. Every movement she makes sends shivers down my spine and I promise myself that I'm going to at least hold her tonight. That is all I want; just to hold her, just to feel her body against mine. That's the other effect she has on me. I might fantasize about her in the shower—I'm only human—but I wouldn't try anything on with her; she's not like Chantal, who'd let anyone lay her for a can of Red Stripe and a few empty words.

My dream girl digs Katia in the ribs. 'You and your "try some of this Polish stuff"—it's gone straight to my head!'

Katia puts her hands on her hips. 'Er, I think my actual words were, "have a little sip of this" and not "swig it down in one", lame brain.'

Erin shakes her head and grins. 'Excuse me, young lady, but you added a dare. What your actual actual words were, were: "have a little sip of this *if you dare.*" I always do dares!'

Katia then comes out with, 'Well, if you're that easily led, I dare you to go give Liam's dad a birthday kiss.'

What a sick thought. 'Oi, steady,' I interrupt.

'It's my birthday too,' Tommo brags, draining his glass. 'I dare you to kiss me, Mackiness.'

Erin raises her eyebrows. 'You do? Then pucker up, baby!'

Everyone laughs, including me, as she bends over and plants this whopper on his mouth. It was mildly amusing at first, but then it goes on for too long and I'm wondering how I can split them up without bloodshed, when the music from the disco starts blasting out and Katia squeals that everyone *must* dance.

We form this kind of circle on the dance floor and jig about. I dance like a total jerk and Tommo's not much better but he's blathered so he doesn't care. The DJ's starting with the old stuff now and chucks on 'Never Ever' by All Saints. Erin shouts: 'This is my song!' and belts out the chorus, arms thrashing about all over the place. We all join in, bellowing, at the top of our lungs.

'I'm going to dedicate that song to my dad!' Erin says, laughing her head off at Katia. Tommo grabs Chantal and tells her it's her turn to give him a birthday kiss so they go off by themselves for a smooch and I'm figuring out how to get rid of Katia when Erin pulls me close and whispers, 'I'm going to go have that word with that rude father of yours, Liam, so look after my best friend for me,' and disappears.

I'm confused again by the 'rude father' bit—but I don't have time to catch my breath before the best friend slides her hands inside my jacket and clasps me to her like a purse snapping shut.

'Watch the suit, it's a Ted Baker,' I tell her.

'You can always take it off if you're worried about creasing it.'

'Slow down, girl.'

'I'm not doing slow tonight,' she says, looking straight into my eyes. She's not shy, I'll give her that. A smoochy record comes on. Katia presses herself close and leans her head against my chest. Her hair smells nice—apricots, the only fruit I like. I sway with her for a while, not knowing what else to do. Tommo's over the other side, necking away with Chantal, so at least they can't see me dancing with her. Over Katia's shoulder, Uncle Patrick gives me the thumbs up.

'Take me upstairs, Liam,' Katia whispers.

'What?'

'Take me to your bedroom.'

She pulls me closer, rubbing herself against me. Naturally, the rubbing has an effect on my little soldier and I couldn't move away now if I wanted to. 'Whoa, girl. Be careful what you're saying or I might take you up on it,' I warn her. I'm only kidding, of course. Kidding and a bit bewildered.

'That's the whole idea,' she says. Her voice is soft, sexy even and her hair does smell of apricots but she's also drunk and probably doesn't know what she's saying.

'What would your mummy and daddy say if they could hear you?' I say, trying to make her see sense.

She presses herself closer and sighs heavily as she connects with my little soldier who's doing a full salute in the old boxers. 'Mummy would be proud,' she says, licking my ear.

'Yeah, as if!'

'It's true! She thinks if you want sex you should go

for it, as long as you don't hurt anyone and always use protection.'

'That's very . . . er . . . "groovy baby" of her.'

She tells me to 'shush' and breathes deeply into my neck. A shiver runs down my back and I shudder. Against all odds, I find myself pulling her closer, sniffing her hair, groaning.

She whispers again. 'Liam, I want you. I've fancied you for ages. I'm only asking for one night, please? One short but fantastic night? You, me, and a whole packet of condoms. No commitments, I promise. I just want to be with you once.'

'Why?' I ask, my voice cracking.

'Why not? What's to stop us?'

What's to stop us? Only a hundred guests, including my entire family. Trouble is, the little soldier's on red alert, yelling Go! Go! Go! It's as if it's taken over and I can't think of anything apart from the need to do what it wants. What Katia wants.

'What about Erin?' I manage to mumble.

'Erin?'

'Won't she say anything?'

Katia shrugs her shoulders. 'She'll call me an idiot, I guess.'

'Why?'

'She thinks you're a slime-ball.'

I feel the beer in my stomach churn. 'A slime-ball?' I mutter.

'Mmm,' Katia continues, oblivious to how hurt and angry I feel. 'I don't though. I think you're gorgeous.'

'Well, we'd better show her what a slime-ball can do, hadn't we?' I say. I pull Katia away and walk off. At the door I turn round, to check she's following. I switch on the stair light and head upstairs.

After, Katia goes casually back to the party as if nothing's happened and I follow her down a few minutes afterwards as if nothing's happened. To be honest, I'm not that sure anything has happened. It was all over that quick.

I need a minute to myself before I can face people so I head for the kitchen and pour myself a glass of water. Was that it? Was that sex? It can't have been. It was too . . . too . . . I don't know—too not special . . . too not worth it. I have a glug of water and am surprised to see my hand shaking. I feel like shit but I don't know why. Lads are meant to not care, aren't they? Meant to go round bragging about every bird they've slept with? They're not meant to want to cry. For the first time in my life I feel totally out of my depth.

Chantal enters. I smile because it's nice to see her— a relief, almost. She's familiar and comfortable and I suppose if you were laying bets on who I'd nail first, it would have been her. I'm about to ask her for a dance to take my mind off things when she goes into one—big time. 'Where've you been?' she rasps. Her eyes are flashing fire as she storms up to me and points the neck of a Metz bottle in my chest. 'I said, where've you been?'

I try to laugh, even though my back's digging in to the edge of the sink and I've got a lunatic shouting in my face. This I can do without. 'Chill out, Chan.'

But she is not in a chilling-out mood. The drink's turned her into a possessive freak. 'You've been with her, haven't you? You've been with that Erin! I bet you set Tommo up to dance with me so you could get off with her!'

Unbelievable! 'I don't know what you're talking about,' I tell her.

'Liar! You've been missing, she's still missing. What have you told her? "Come down in five minutes" like you do to me when we're at the Centre so no one knows what you've been up to?'

'Course not.'

I want to tell her it's not like that at all. I want to ask her to give me a hug like she does to Morgan when he's fretting but I can't do that, can I? Because she's looking at me now and thinking the same thing Erin does. Slime-ball.

'Liar! Bloody liar!' she shouts. 'Still, I suppose you don't mind people knowing you've been with *her*. You're not ashamed of *her*, are you? She's good enough to be seen in public with, isn't she? Just cos she's blonde. We can all do blonde, you know!'

The girl's so in my face I can see the blackheads on her chin. 'You've got it all wrong, Chan, totally.'

But she's deaf to whatever I say. This whole evening is turning into a nightmare. 'You're supposed to be going out with me! You said so on Wednesday! You said you loved me!' she raves, then her face crumples and I know she's trying not to cry but I'm not admitting to something so radical, even though part of it's true. 'I never said I loved you, Chan, and you know it.'

She chucks the bottle at me but I catch it easily, luckily for her. 'You did, you lying git!' she yells, ' . . . behind the fire exit when you had your hand down my bra!'

'Shurrup!' I bark at her in case someone hears. She starts crying then and flings her bony arms round my neck. I try to prise her off but she's got a grip tighter than a knot in a balloon. 'C'mon, Chantal, you know what I'm like. You shouldn't take me seriously,' I tell her.

She lets go and stares at me with hurt, watery eyes. 'I just want to know where I stand with you, that's all.'

Normally, I would have laughed in her face. Well, it's such a corny line, isn't it? But for once I understand how it feels to be used, because that's what the episode upstairs feels like. That I've just been used by Katia so she could get what she always wanted without any strings attached. I've been using Chantal like that for months.

I look at the poor bint waiting desperately opposite me. I squint beneath the savage make-up that hardens her face and find a young lass trying to grow up too fast. A lass who thinks if you do what lads want, they'll love you for it. She hasn't learned, yet, despite her sister Nicola's mistake, that she'll get the opposite. I feel a lump harden in my throat because I feel sorry for the pair of us. 'What are you looking at me like that for?' she asks, all narked.

Gently, I fold my arms around her and tell her I'm sorry. She sniffs loudly in my ear. 'So are we officially going out then?' she asks gruffly, fumbling with one hand to reach her mobile.

I try to think of something that won't hurt her, something that sounds real. I tell her quickly, I tell her straight. 'No. I like you, Chan, but I don't want to go out with you. I've known you all my life, right? You feel more like a sister to me—I want to be able to talk to you about stuff like I do Tommo, like mates. I wouldn't be able to do that if I was dating you, would I?'

'What about at the Centre? You don't treat me like a sister then, do you?' she snarls as the mobile is pushed roughly back into her bag.

'That's not going to happen again,' I tell her straight. And I mean it. I am not ever going to lose my virginity again until my wedding night. Fact.

'Yeah, right, till next time,' she says sarcastically.

'No, I'm serious, Chan. I want to wait until I meet the right person for all that—like my mam and dad did. You should, too—have a bit of respect for yourself, like.'

Chantal digs a finger repeatedly into my chest. 'Who do you think you are, talking to me about respect? I get respect, thank you very much. There's loads of lads think I'm all right! You're not the only "fit bit" on the estate, tosser!'

'Don't get mad,' I beg her but she's gone into a massive strop, staring blankly out of the window. Playing games.

I've had enough of this party now. All I want to do is go upstairs and sleep. I'm about to tell Chantal so when Erin rushes past, her face screwed up and pale. Chantal immediately lunges for me again and starts kissing my neck. I strain to see where Erin's gone when Tommo flies through saying 'Hang on, hang on,' but Erin yanks open the back door and dashes out. I ask Tommo what's going on but he just mutters something about not worrying, he'll handle it, and goes after her. I try to break free but Chantal's still locked-on, beaming all over. 'Looks like blondes don't have all the fun, then,' she says, happily dragging me towards the dance floor.

By half three there's only the hardened crew remaining in the corner of the marquee. Uncle Patrick walked Chantal and a few others from the estate back about an hour ago and now wants to set up an arm wrestling league. Cork versus Kilkenny.

I watch with a fake smile on my face as Auntie Orla (Cork) rolls up her sleeves and takes two seconds to beat Uncle Patrick. I laugh out loud, as I'm expected to do. 'You're next, Liam,' Auntie Orla shouts but I just tell her I don't want to hurt her and wander back to the kitchen to find Tommo. I need to talk to him, bad. But Tommo's spark out, head resting on the table, the empty bottle of Jack Daniels nearby. I envy him.

Dad's sitting opposite, a cup of black coffee in one hand, prawn vol-au-vent in the other. 'All right?' he asks me.

'Great. You?'

He shrugs, undoing his collar. 'I suppose so. I'd have been just as happy with a pint at The Queen's Head but don't tell your mother that.'

'I won't.'

Dad leans across and rubs my hair. 'You look shattered. Too much strutting your stuff, eh!'

'Strutting my stuff'? Where does he get them from? 'Yeah, right.'

'Just remember that talk I gave you the other week, boyo, that's all. Make sure the three minutes is worth it.'

How does he do that? How does he know exactly the worst thing to say to me? It's Mam who's supposed to be psychic. 'Yeah, Dad, thanks. It's nice of you to keep bringing it up. I appreciate it, like,' I say calm as you like. He laughs but a feeling of misery swamps me again when I think of the sex with Katia because I know he's right. The three minutes wasn't worth it.

'Dad?'

'Mm.'

'Were you a virgin before you married Mam?'

'Course I was.'

'Honest?'

He looks me straight in the eye and says, 'How could I not be? I was only seventeen when I met her. She was only fifteen, remember. We'd both have had something to say to each other if we hadn't been.' *Only* seventeen? I'm not even fifteen until June.

'What about Uncle Patrick? He's been married twice, so he can't have been a virgin the second time round. How does that fit in with the rules?'

'Everyone's entitled to one mistake, son. And that first wife of his was one big mistake!'

I grin but wonder how much deeper I can afford to

prod without him getting suspicious. 'Don't you ever wonder what it'd be like with someone else?'

He frowns into his coffee. 'No, not really. What you've never had you never miss.'

'Have you never been tempted? There must have been someone you've looked at and thought she's a bit of all right, just for a one-night stand or something—before you got married, like.'

Dad leans back in his chair and scowls. 'Maybe,' he shrugs, 'maybe once or twice but just because I'm looking at the menu it doesn't mean I want to eat, does it? Anyway, why the sudden interest in my love life?'

'Dunno. We can go on to football now, if you like.'

'Thanks, son,' he says with relief.

We rabbit on about Forest's chances against City tomorrow but I'm not really concentrating. All I can think of is that I'll never be able to tell my kid that I was a virgin when I met his mam.

I need Tommo awake. I need to tell him what's happened. Tommo's top man when it comes to sorting out problems—he'll know what to do. I tap him on the bonce with an empty tube of Pringles.

'Leave the poor lad alone. He'll have a bad enough head in the morning,' Dad says.

'That's his fault.'

Dad drains his coffee, looks thoughtful. 'That Erin's a bit intense, isn't she?' he suddenly says.

My heart starts pounding. Even though she thinks I'm scum, I still quake when I hear her name. 'What? What do you mean?'

And he starts telling me about this letter she'd written to him about that table we'd bought off them that time. 'Started crying and going on and on when I told her I'd sold it weeks ago. Said she was looking for a Saturday job and would give me her fifty quid Christmas money from her gran when she got it, as a deposit. Poor lass. I didn't tell her she'd need ten times that much to buy that piece back, even if I hadn't sold it. Told her I didn't know anything about a letter.' He glances at me, then looks down. We both know that anything that's not an invoice, that's out of the ordinary so his secretary can't deal with it, would have gone straight in the bin. If it's urgent, they'll phone, is his way of looking at things. 'She'd had too much to drink. You start far too young, these days,' he finishes lamely, picking up the empty whisky bottle and squinting at the label.

So that's what all the fuss had been about. All the 'words with your rude dad' malarkey. Why hadn't she come to me? Why didn't she tell me about the table? I could have sorted it.

I pictured her, flinging her arms round my neck and kissing me, kissing me the way she'd kissed Tommo, as I showed her the table I'd had removed to the storerooms, protected with a tarpaulin with a 'not for sale' sticker on top of it. I'd have been *so* flavour of Mackiness's month. I wouldn't have been a slime-ball, then, would I?

Dad's about to add something when there's an almighty clatter on the back door. 'What the—?' he asks and leaps up.

The night air blows in with Mr Boyle's whiny voice. 'Is my lad in there, Tony? Is he?'

Tommo stirs and groans at the sound of his dad's words. 'Tell him to go home,' he grumbles.

But Dad does the opposite and invites him in for a coffee. Mr Boyle refuses. 'No, thanks, Tony. I've just come to see if I can wish my own flesh and blood a happy birthday.' He sounds totally hammered, which is nothing new. What is new is him turning up here.

'Tell him to go. Dad, it's freezing with that door open,' I hiss.

'It's all right, I'll leave,' Tommo says, slowly unfolding himself like a clapped-out deckchair.

'No, don't. You're sleeping over, remember.'

Tommo shrugs, bleary eyed. 'Makes no difference, does it, and it'll keep the peace.' His voice is flat as if he's too tired to argue.

Dad's trying to persuade Tommo's dad to leave him until morning, even says if he comes in, he'll call for a cab, or he could kip down in the living room. Then Benny gets embarrassing, and starts crying. Honest. The full works. His voice comes through all dramatic and emotional. 'No, Tony, no. It's Thomas I want, that's all; he's all I've got left now. Are you there, son? I just want to share the day with you. Come home with me, please, son, please.' What a nerve. The guy hasn't even bought him a present and now he's giving it all this.

Dad goes to call for a cab anyway and I go to the window and see Mr Boyle stumble over one of Mam's Grecian urns. He's in a right state, cursing and gobbing and crying all at the same time. Pathetic. You'd never guess he went to university once, would you? My dad would never, ever do anything so uncool.

'I'm nothing without you, Thomas, nothing!' the guy blubs.

'You can say that again, loser,' I mutter under my breath.

'He is a loser,' Tommo says from behind me, 'but he's all I've got.'

I twirl round to apologize but he's already got his jacket on. Or trying to. He's getting it all twisted and he's going to rip the lining if he's not careful so I lean forward to help but he shrugs me away, dead narked. 'Leave it!' he says sharply. 'It's not *designer*; I don't want you to soil your hands or anything.'

'That's a bit harsh, Tommo.'

He snarls at me. 'Harsh? You haven't got a clue about harsh.' Then he's gone.

I don't sleep very well. There's no smell of apricots but there's a mark on the sheet I'm going to find hard to explain if Mam sees it. I lie on top of the bed and wish I had got ratted.

I'm glad next morning I have the match to take my mind off things. It's only a kick-about, really, with some lads from our Youth Centre against another centre. We should have thrashed them but I just can't get my act together. By half-time I've lost interest and ask to be subbed. No one objects.

It's still only mid-morning. At home, I know I'd only get roped in to helping clear up so I head for Tommo's. I guess he'll still be zonked from the party but I want to talk to him anyway. We've got stuff that needs sorting.

I don't want to fall out with him, he's my best mate, but he needs to be put right about one or two things. '*It's not designer.*' What was that supposed to mean? And me not knowing what harsh was. 'Hey, Tommo,' I'll tell him, 'I get the impression you think I'm a spoilt twat, that we've all got it easy in our house. Well, you're wrong. My dad's worked hard for what he's got, fifteen hours a day sometimes, building up a business from scratch, taking the flak from both sides. First from travellers having a go at him, telling him he's a traitor because he won't buy their dodgy antiques, then from coppers who keep turning his shops over every time there's a burglary. *That Droy must be bent, mustn't he, if he's a gyppo?* He couldn't win, Tommo. But he stuck to it, didn't sort his problems out by getting paralytic like Benny.

'And what about my mam? I wasn't meant to be an only child, you know, mate. Three miscarriages Mam had before I came along. Three, including one at six months. Janine. Baby Janine. She'd have been seventeen by now. So, course I'm spoilt. Why not? And by the way, you drink too much, Tommo. You're gonna end up just like him, so watch it.'

I walk faster, thinking, Liam man, that is one fine speech you are going to deliver. I reach the beginning of his road when a cab with a shot exhaust pulls up next to me. The geezer winds down the window and asks me for Quarry Rise. 'Been to Quarry Bank, Quarry Road, Quarry Close,' he complains.

'You're on it,' I tell him, 'this is Quarry Rise.'

'Cheers, son,' he says as the car slowly rattles ahead.

He stops at the end, outside Tommo's. 'You could have given me a lift,' I joke, wondering who wants a taxi in that joint at this time of day. 'I'll tell them you're here,' I say. 'Who do you want?'

'Mr Boyle for the station.'

'Right.'

They never lock their door, so I go straight in. You can't move in their hallway for books; shelves and shelves of them, all old and dusty and depressing.

Quickly, I push past them, and follow the sound of the Hoover into the front room. It's Benny in his overcoat, vaccing away. The room's spotless and so's he, amazingly—clean-shaven and smartly dressed—you would never have known it was the same guy from a few hours ago. That's what's confusing about alkies—rock bottom one minute, full of the joys the next. 'Your cab's here,' I shout above the racket.

He gives me this gigantic grin, switches the machine off and begins winding the flex round the handle. He's trying to do it quickly and making a right hash of it. In the end he just bundles the whole thing round the back of the armchair and disappears through into the dining room.

Seconds later he comes back in with a carrier bag

full of stuff; there's a jitteriness about him that I can't quite suss. 'Going somewhere nice?' I ask.

'I am, Liam,' he beams, 'and if everything turns out as planned, it's going to be a momentous day for all of us. Is my tie straight?' he finishes.

I tell him yes, his tie is straight and ask if I can go up and see Tommo but he's halfway down the path already.

Tommo's bedroom is a pit. It's dark and stinks and I just don't know how he lives in it. He's lying face to the wall, his duvet pulled over his head. I shake him, really hard, just to annoy him and yell in his ear-hole. He doesn't answer but pulls his legs up, making himself smaller. His whole body is trembling. 'What's up? Bit of a hangover?'

What's up is that he's crying. I haven't seen him cry since Year Eight when he got a cricket ball in his nads. 'I told him, Liam, I told him,' he sobs.

'Told who what?'

'Told Benny where Mum and the kids are.'

I let the news sink in. 'Look, he was bound to find out sooner or later, wasn't he? It's not your fault.'

He struggles to sit up but almost faints with the effort. His words are garbled and I find it difficult to understand what he's on about. 'I promised her, I promised her I wouldn't tell but we started talking last night, me and Dad, really deep stuff and I ended up revealing where she was. I thought he'd forget about it but no, it has to be the one time he remembers something after the night before. He's on his way there now . . .'

I try to be positive. 'Come on, Tommo, you know the score—Benny'll drop in to the Station Tavern for a swift half and end up on a bender round town and that'll be that.'

Tommo shakes his head vigorously then winces with pain. 'Don't underestimate him—he's totally determined. He thinks all he has to do is turn up and she'll see sense and we can be a family again. We were never a family! He forgets . . . he forgets how scathing she is of him. And when she starts belittling him, mocking him for "lowering himself" to her level when he married her and teasing him with what-could-have-beens, it winds him up, of course, because she never knows when to stop, then he loses it and she gets scared and that makes him even worse because he doesn't understand what she has to be scared about. And then . . .' he trails off.

I know, Tommo, I know. Then he beats the crap out of her. Mam's told me even if you haven't. I'm trying hard to think of something soothing to say. 'They won't let him in the refuge, though, even if he finds her, will they? I thought you said it was all security locked and that.'

Tommo lets out this long, exasperated breath. 'But he'll know where it is, won't he? It won't be a *refuge* for her any more, pillock.'

'Well, they must have phones or faxes in these places. Can't you just call your mam and warn her?'

He wipes his eyes on the back of his hand. 'I could . . . I ought to but . . . but she'll do a runner again and this time she won't tell me where she's going. I'll never see them again, Liam, never and I couldn't stand it. I miss Jimmy and Sarah like mad. If I can get to her first, and explain . . .'

He's squeezing his eyes shut in pain. I've never seen him like this and it cuts me up. I have to help him. I get out the mobile and phone for Mam to pick us up, explaining what was happening as best I could. Instant earache. '*Where* is this refuge?' she bleats.

'Stirling.'

'In Scotland?'

'No, in Tinkywinky Land,' I wisecrack. Full-blown stress-out on the other end of the line. 'But your dad's gone with Uncle Patrick and everyone to Southwell Races and you know I can't drive on motorways. I just can't!' Mam squawks.

'Mam, if we don't get there before Benny . . . '

'I know, I know,' she snaps, 'I took Gayle to casualty last time, didn't I? Just give me a minute to think.'

'We haven't got a minute!' I yell.

The line goes dead. Tommo comes in, sees my face and shrugs, 'It was a lame idea anyway but thanks for trying.'

I feel miserable because I've let him down so soon. I make him a cup of tea while he gets dressed. Downstairs, he stares at the phone on his lap, building up courage to ring the refuge. 'At least he didn't get the number out of me,' he says, dialling the first digit. He is interrupted by a horn blasting outside the house. The cavalry has arrived.

It's Mam all right but she's with Mrs Mackiness and Erin in their joke space wagon. Mam quickly explains that Sue has agreed to drive us, though how she expects us to get to Stirling in that thing before a 125 I do not know.

We pile in. I leave Tommo to give all the details. Erin's told to phone the station and find out train times and Mam's made to trace the route to Stirling (big mistake but I keep out of it). Mrs Mack nods. 'We should be able to beat him. Even if he caught the 11.59 he has to change at York and Edinburgh. I still think you ought to phone the refuge, though, Tom, to warn your mother.'

Tommo shakes his head and he explains why he can't, his voice coming out like broken glass.

'Might she not move on afterwards without you anyway?' she says. It's a harsh question but she asks it gently.

Tommo shrugs. 'I'll risk it.'

Mrs Mack exchanges a look with Mam and puts the key in the ignition and we're off. We settle down. Mam and Mrs Mack up front, Tommo, Erin, and me at the back with a row of empty seats in between. 'Hiya,' I say to Erin.

'Hi,' she answers.

'Good game, eh?'

She frowns. I've said the wrong thing. A typical slime-ball's thing.

Tommo's gone into himself, staring out of the window; not answering when I ask him something.

It's going to be a long journey.

12

We arrive on Linden Street, where the refuge is supposed to be, just after five. Benny's train is due in at 5.15, providing he's caught it, of course. We'll know soon enough. Mrs Mack circles the street about six times trying to park but it's a busy road with spaces for permit holders only. In the end, Tommo, Mam, and me jump out while Mrs Mack and Erin find somewhere to dump the wagon.

Each house on Linden Street is three storeys high in black stone with colossal front doors like something out of *The Addams Family*. The refuge has got one of those intercom things on the front, otherwise it looks exactly like all the others. Tommo presses it but Mam holds him back, says it might be better if she talks, being a woman. This deep Scottish voice comes crackling back with about a dozen questions. What feels like a year later, there's another voice, and it's Tommo's mam. 'Mum, it's me,' Tommo says into the box, his voice all kind of spindly and I know he's scared and chuffed at the same time.

The door opens slightly and Mrs Boyle appears. Her eyes dart to Tommo and she gasps and shrieks, all happy, but Mam almost pushes her back inside. 'You wait for Sue and Erin,' she tells me and disappears, banging the door shut. Charming, I think, but I know she has no choice, really. There's a McDonald's across the road and I head for that, intending to stand near the entrance and wave the Mackinesses over when I see them. I dodge the traffic and push open the heavy glass door.

The brilliant thing about McDonald's is they're all the same so it doesn't matter if you're in Scotland or Saudi, you always feel at home. My stomach growls at the familiar smell but I tell myself it would look bad tucking in to a Big Mac Meal with all the drama going on across the way. Instead I decide on a trip to the bog but I only get as far as the plastic yukka plant near the entrance to the toilets when a hand shoots out and grabs me. 'Good evening, Liam,' Mr Boyle says.

I nearly have a heart attack on the spot. 'All right?' I mumble.

'All right?' he snorts, staring into his plastic coffee cup. 'What do you think?' He pulls out a stool, inviting me to join him. I wonder whether to do a runner but I reckon there are enough customers to help if he starts anything. Besides, if he's in here he can't be causing any hassle across the way, so I give myself the job of stalling him for as long as I can. Slowly, I take a pew, keeping my eyes fixed on his, assessing him.

He isn't sloshed—at least I don't think he is, but the mega-fine mood from this morning has disappeared; now he just looks tired out and a bit confused. I can risk five minutes.

'Were you on the train too? I never saw you,' he says, as if it were the most normal thing in the world that I would have been on it. 'Ten minutes early, eh? Who would have credited it?'

'Yeah—amazing.'

'Thomas is with his mother, I presume.'

We both glance through the window to the gloomy house opposite. It's pitch black now but there isn't much light coming from the refuge. Mr Boyle covers my hand with his; it's cold and rough but his grip is loose so I know I can pull away any time I want. I look at him and see his eyes are full of tears but I don't pity him. I know it sounds hard but I've seen it all before. He lets the tears fall, dripping like rain into his collar. 'I love them all, Liam, I really do—I never planned for it to turn out like this.'

'I guess not.'

'Life's hard, you know.'

'Yeah, I know.'

He lets out this long, deep sigh and it annoys me, the way Tommo annoyed me at the end of the party last night. It's like Dad says, if people stopped whinging on and did something about their lives they wouldn't have to live like dossers. Not that Mr Boyle's a dosser, exactly, but you'd think he'd get his act together with three kids to support.

'What are you going to do?' I ask, trying to sound him out.

He casts his eyes towards the refuge and shrugs. 'Look at it, Liam, look at that place. To think she prefers to hole up like a prisoner in that gothic monstrosity than live with me. Was she so desperate?'

More tears spill down his face. From his pocket, he pulls a nearly empty quart bottle of vodka and I realize he is sauced after all. Clever, of course, because vodka doesn't smell the breath up. After a quick gulp, he slides it back, glancing quickly towards the supervisor at the counter in case he's been sussed. 'It's all my fault. We should never have got married. I wanted to be really working class to fit in with my "Socialist Worker" image so I married Gayle. It was all crap, really. I was just punishing my parents. That's all the young ever do, isn't it? Punish their parents? Eh, Liam?'

'If you say so, Mr Boyle.'

'They were very posh, you know, or thought they were. I bet that surprises you, doesn't it? Me having posh parents? Do you know where I met her?'

'Who?'

'Gayle. My wife. My awful wedded wife.'

I shook my head. I didn't really want to know but he was going to tell me anyway.

'She was behind the counter at the off-licence. A checkout girl. Perfect! And she was so impressed with me. A real student! Fancy that! I . . . I never planned for it to turn out like this,' he repeats.

'Yeah. You said.'

He nods enthusiastically and starts hammering on about how his mother was an alcoholic and his father was a philanderer and how he wished he hadn't dropped out of university after only a term because of naive, misplaced ideologies. I try to listen but my stomach's rumbling with hunger and all I can think of is a Big Mac. Then he starts on about addictive personality disorders or something but he's lost me halfway through and I begin staring at the menu above the counter instead.

'Are you hungry?' he says, breaking off when he sees I'm not listening. He pulls out a crumpled fiver from inside his coat and slides it towards me. 'Go on,' he says, 'take it. I'll have another coffee.'

I chance it. No one's waiting so I get served straight away and I'm back within a minute. I hand him his coffee and change. He nods, leaving the coins on the table between us. 'What would you do, Liam?' he asks.

'What, if I were you?'

'Yes, if you were me.'

'I'd forget about it, Mr Boyle. I'd just go home and get some kip.'

He leans his head to one side, as if he's considering it. 'Well, that's one idea, I suppose. Alternatively, I could just go across and strangle the neurotic bitch. That'll put us all out of our misery.'

He howls with laughter at me, knowing I can't work out if he's winding me up or what. 'Eat your food,' he says as he takes another sly gulp from his bottle, 'it'll go cold.' His eyes are all over the place, darting out of the window, then back to me, down to my untouched burger, back to the window. 'Ha! If only you knew the half of it, Liam. If only you knew the half. Thomas is over there, you said?'

I nod.

'Who else?'

'My mum.'

'And Tony?'

I tell him yes, thinking I'd better because I'm on edge again. Boyle nods. 'He's a good man, your father. You're a lucky lad.'

'I know.'

Thomas's dad looks at me for a long, long time, forcing me to look back. The stare feels like a challenge; the goalie against the penalty taker. 'You don't rate me, much, do you, son?' he says eventually.

I don't answer.

There's a pause that seems to go on forever when, without warning, the guy leans across and kisses me on the head. 'Give that to Thomas for me, tell him thanks for sticking by me . . . tell him . . . tell him I love him.'

He's got no chance—I don't say soft stuff like that. 'Where are you going?' I ask. He's standing up, using the stem of the yukka plant for support. He digs into his coat again and I presume he's going for the vodka but he throws down a bunch of keys. They land on top of his change with a clank. 'Tell Gayle she can have the house back, she can have everything. I promise I won't be back. I mean it. I won't be back, if that's what it takes to make her and the kids happy. I've put her through enough.'

'Where are you going?' I ask him again.

He turns and shrugs. 'God knows,' he says, and staggers out.

* * *

Tommo's just gazing at the keys in his hand. 'Are you sure?' he says to me, 'are you positive?' He's sitting opposite me in McDonald's, their Sarah on his knee, Jimmy hunched up next to him, tucking into a milk shake. Erin and her mam are on the next table, talking quietly, glancing across now and again. My mam's still with Mrs Boyle in the refuge, discussing what to do next. Mrs Boyle's taking some persuading that Benny means it this time, that he's serious. So is Tommo, but it's hard to tell how he feels about it.

'Sure I'm sure,' I repeat for about the millionth time. 'He promised he wouldn't be back.' I don't tell him about the kiss—I don't want to embarrass the guy.

'Does that mean I can go back to Miss Purnell's class, Tom?' Sarah asks. She's eight, with a crooked front tooth and hair that curls all round her long, thin face.

'Yeah,' he says in a flat voice, 'I guess.'

'Good,' Sarah replies.

Mrs Boyle's not having any of it, though. When we return the kids to the refuge, she just smiles tightly for half a second and backs away into the dark hallway before Mam has a chance to finish pressing money into the kids' hands. 'I'm not making any decisions until I've seen my counsellor,' Tommo's mam snaps at him when he asks her if she'll be home this week. I notice for the first time she's had her nose pierced and her hair cropped. It's not a good look for someone the wrong side of forty but each to their own, I suppose. 'I'll call you,' she says, closing the door firmly in our faces.

'Your dad's broken his word so many times, she just doesn't trust him any more,' Mam says quietly, trying to explain, as we all clamber in the back of Erin's Espace. 'Give her time, Tommy, she needs to build her confidence back up again, pet. You can stay with us for as long as you like, you know that, don't you?'

Tommo nods but doesn't say thanks or anything but I know he's grateful underneath.

'What are you going to do?' Erin asks Tommo.

'Sleep,' he says.

'Lean on me, if you want to,' she invites and he does. I try not to care, especially as he's asleep within seconds, stretched across her lap as if it was the most normal thing in the world and not something I would give my left arm for. Still, I've got no chance, have I? I'm just a slime-ball, aren't I?

'It puts things into perspective, doesn't it, something like this?' Erin whispers to me.

'What do you mean?'

'Well, I thought I had problems but they're nothing compared to Tom's.'

I shrug, not knowing what to say. 'Did your dad tell you about the table?' she whispers, checking over my shoulder in case the oldies at the front hear. She's no need to worry—that pair won't stop talking until they're back home in their own beds.

'Yeah, he mentioned something.'

'I feel like such an idiot. Will you tell him I'm sorry for making a scene on his birthday?'

'Forget about it.'

'I had too much to drink. I felt so foul this morning. Katia was worse than me—I couldn't even wake her to say goodbye when we left. She'll be fuming when she wakes up.'

I couldn't care less but I asked why anyway.

'Knowing I've spent the day with you. She thinks you're wonderful, if you hadn't already guessed.'

I look at her, to see if there's any hidden meaning behind her words but she's smiling lightly. 'Sorry,' she says, glancing down at Tommo. 'I know it's probably not the right time but I kind of promised her before the party I'd ask you if you'd go out with her then it all went a bit loopy and I never got round to it.'

'What else did she say?' I ask, my voice barely audible.

Erin leaned closer. 'What?'

'What else did she say last night—after the party?' I ask.

'Nothing—she was too busy throwing up! Why?'

'Nothing.'

I shake my head and turn away. This is one bizarre mess of a weekend. It is like one of those sequencing exercises we used to do in English where you have rows of sentences that are all jumbled up and you have to cut them out and stick them in the right order. That's what I want to do now. I want to swap everything round so that under the heading 'My Weekend' it read: 1) Went to Dad's party; 2) Danced all night with Erin; 3) Tommo's dad called round for a nice chat and caught a taxi home; 4) Asked Erin out—she said yes—the end.

But then I wake up and it's all a dream.

'Liam,' Erin says, nudging me on my shoulder.

'What?'

'I just want to say I thought you were brilliant today.'

'What do you mean?' I ask, not turning round.

'The way you handled Mr Boyle. That can't have been easy.'

'Yeah, well.'

'Tom's lucky to have you and your mum and dad supporting him.'

'That's what friends are for, isn't it?' I twist round, surprised to find her so close, her arms lying across my backrest, Tommo flat out across the seats behind her. Any closer and our noses would have been touching. I pull back. 'Well, you've done your bit. You didn't have to drive all this way with your mam.'

'Course we did. Remember that time at the hospital with Nina?'

'It's not the same.'

'It's just the same. We're neighbours, right? That's what neighbours do.'

'Even if you think they're slime-balls?'

Erin looks startled, then grins. 'You've been reading my writing in the girls' toilets again, haven't you?'

'Don't deny it, then!' I tell her, trying to keep it light, codding her I don't care. I can take it. I'm Liam Droy, cool guy, aren't I?

She buys it, laughing gently at me. 'OK, I admit I may have used the words "slime-ball", "pig", and "conceited moron" to describe you in the past but I wouldn't now.'

'You wouldn't?' I ask huskily, moving slightly closer. We stare at each other for ages and there's a connection, I know there is.

Her eyes dart to my neck then back to my eyes, then she clears her throat and shuffles back to her seat next to Tommo. 'You don't have to give me an answer straight away about Katia. Just promise you'll think about it, huh?'

'Oh, sure,' I reply.

The next couple of weeks are dead weird. It should have been brilliant, having Tommo stay. A right lark. But he's wound up and edgy all the time, waiting. Waiting for Benny to come back, waiting for his mam to call. Benny doesn't come back. Gayle doesn't call.

I don't know what the big deal is. Mrs B's been away for ages anyway—it's not as if he doesn't know where she is. And Benny's gone AWOL tons of times but he always comes back, when he remembers where he lives. If it were me, I'd just relax and enjoy the freedom and the decent grub.

Instead, Tommo begins to spend more and more time at Quarry Rise, sorting things out, keeping the house in order. I go round with him after school but the place has that cold, unlived-in feel to it so I never stay long and usually end up coming home on my tod.

School's weird, too. I'm moved back to Mme Crecy's

in French but Tommo gets to stay with Blackhead. 'You're surprisingly showing potential, Thomas,' Mr Whitehead told him, 'we'll keep you with us a little longer and see what happens.' In one way, I'm relieved. It means I don't have to face Katia; though to be honest, she's packed in those long, lingering looks she used to give me every time we passed in the corridor. If I'm dead honest, she's ignoring me as much as I'm ignoring her. I get the impression that if I did ask her out, which obviously, I never would, she'd say no. Chantal's the same. Won't even speak to me at the Centre. Turns her back and makes out she's engrossed in some deep conversation with Erica every time I pass. Well, they can all go to hell for all I care. Except for Erin and Tommo, of course, though Tommo's round her house doing French homework a bit too often for my liking; but there's nothing I can do about it, is there? They're just mates, right?

It's two weeks before Christmas. Everyone's in the kitchen. I'm up a ladder at one end. Dad's up a ladder at the other end. Between us, there's a string of plastic reindeer lights that we're trying to drape above Jesus, Diana, and Elvis. Below me, Tommo's huddled over the kitchen table with Mam, showing her this letter from the council. Their rent's in arrears and he's worried about losing the house. Mam tuts and shakes her head. She's been getting a bit frustrated with Gayle Boyle's parenting skills lately. No phone call in days. 'You'll have to forward it to your mum, love. She's going to have to come back and sort things out. It's not up to you.'

'Dad's always paid the rent on time, always,' Tommo mutters.

'Oh, now what?' Dad says, craning his neck behind me.

I twist round to see two coppers walking up the path. 'Fiver says break-in at the Carver Street shop,' I say to Dad.

He clambers down the ladder and makes for the door before the coppers can reach the bell. It's one of each. At least I think it is. The female copper's well in need of a bit of Immac on her upper lip. They're invited in and stand in the doorway blinking for a second at the bright light while they make their introductions. 'Is it one of the burglar alarms?' Dad asks.

'Er . . . no, Mr Droy,' the woman constable says, 'I'm afraid not.'

And she looks at Tommo.

'Local Man Found Dead in Scottish River' was how our paper phrased it. Good one, Benny. Nice Christmas present for the kids, mate.

ERIN

'Put some cling-film over the trifle, Georgia,' Mum ordered, 'and Nina, stop picking your new nail—it will never form properly at this rate—and go get ready.'

Nina looked up guiltily from the table and hid her hands behind her back. 'Shall I make a card?'

'I suppose you can, if you're quick,' Mum muttered as Nina scooted off, 'and Erin . . . '

I gripped my magazine tighter. Don't start on me, woman, I thought to myself, just because you've got us all invited to something nobody wants to go to and now you're in a flap about it.

'Erin,' Mum repeated.

'Yes, mother dear?'

'Tell your dad to hurry up.'

'He's setting the video for *It's a Wonderful Life*,' Georgia informed us. Good one, sis—rub it in that Dad would be missing his favourite film of all time to spend Boxing Day over at the Droys'.

Mum sighed heavily. 'Do you think we should have bought them presents?' she said, half to herself.

'Who?' Georgia asked.

'The Boyle children.'

'Will they have bought us any?' Georgia asked reasonably.

Mum frowned. 'No, of course not but that's not the point. Maybe I should just pop out to Quarishi's and get them a big tube of Skittles or fruit pastilles each or something.'

Time to intervene. 'Mum, stop fussing, they've got more to worry about than fruit pastilles,' I said levelly.

'Yeah,' Georgia agreed, a sombre look on her face, 'because if my dad had died near Christmas I wouldn't want any sweets. I probably wouldn't eat my Christmas dinner, either—not all of it, anyway. Definitely not the chipolatas, because they're his favourite. I'd probably look at the chipolatas and start crying and crying until I thought I was going to drown in my own tears.'

'Nice allusion, Georgie—very subtle.'

'What?'

I raised one newly-plucked eyebrow. 'Drowning?'

'Oh God,' Mum said, tying her hair back into a loose ponytail, 'it's going to be a disaster, isn't it?'

'Yep,' I said helpfully.

'I only agreed to go because I felt sorry for Bonita. She invited Gayle and the children over because she thought they might need a bit of company after all they've been through.'

'And we were invited because?'

Mum chewed her lip. 'She thought it would be nice for all the children to play together.'

'I don't want to play with them. I don't know them,' Georgia declared.

126

'And I don't want to play with them because I do know them,' I added, 'and I'm staying at Katia's tonight, remember, so I don't want to be late.'

Mum smiled tightly at us both. 'Now come on, you two, a couple of hours isn't going to hurt, is it?'

It was cold and drizzling outside as we wordlessly trailed round to the Droys', armed with a bottle of red wine and the sherry trifle. 'It's not going to be all emotional, is it?' Dad asked plaintively as we waited for the door to open.

'For God's sake, Noel!' Mum snapped. 'Show some compassion.'

'Yeah, Dad, show some compassion, for God's sake,' I grinned at him.

Dad was better at taking cheek since he'd been given a temporary six month contract with the council. It was nothing like his old job, money-wise, but he came home a different person in the evenings—more *Dad-like*. He moaned about how untidy we were, he complained that we always ate the biscuits before he got any, he asked if we'd done homework, and worst of all, he passed on really bad jokes he'd heard from 'the lads'. We were beginning to gel again.

The one thing he was never very good at though, even in The Lodge, was mixing at things like this. It wasn't that he was anti-social, it was just that, well, he preferred watching *It's a Wonderful Life*. Making small talk with the recently bereaved was not his forte.

'They must all be in the back,' Mum said brightly, moving towards the doorbell again. As she did so, the door was flung open by Mrs Droy, a halo of tinsel around her head and huge snowmen earrings dangling from her ears. Her accessories still did nothing to distract from her ever-exposed boobs which she had dosed liberally with body glitter. I tried not to laugh as I saw Dad hastily avert his eyes as she wrapped her arms around him. 'Noel! Sue! Merry Christmas—or is it too late for that? I'm never sure—it never seems to end, does it? Come in! Come in!'

'How's everything going?' Mum whispered as we followed her through the hallway.

'Oh, brilliant. They've put Gayle on anti-depressants so she's very well, considering they've still got the main inquest to come. Very . . . er . . . cheerful, you might say.'

'Oh, that's good,' Mum said, not daring to make eye contact with Dad.

In the living room, Mrs Boyle was scrunched tightly into one corner of the vast sofa, a drink in one hand, newly lit cigarette in the other. Mr Droy, who had just finished pouring himself a drink from the 'cocktail bar', looked up and smiled and said hello but Mrs Boyle just glanced at us then focused on her glass. James and Sarah, the little kids I'd seen briefly in McDonald's, were hunched up in front of the television, watching cartoons. 'Liam and Tommy are playing pool if you want to go through,' Mrs Droy informed us over-zealously, as if she had made the offer of a lifetime.

We all stood, unsure of what to do for a second, until Nina pulled out a folded piece of paper from under her jumper and handed it to Sarah. 'I've made you a card,' she said to Sarah, who frowned.

'That's nice,' Mrs Droy said, smiling with relief at this instant ice-breaker. 'What does it say, chicken?'

Sarah held open the card, frowning even harder. I wasn't surprised. Nina's handwriting was still at the circles and stick stage. 'It says: sorry your dad's dead,' Sarah announced solemnly.

Mum coughed and whispered 'oh dear'. There was a crack of laughter from the sofa. We turned to see Mrs Boyle, almost doubled up in hysterics and trying hard not to spill her drink. She reminded me of a bad actress, hamming it up for the audience. 'Sorry he's dead? Well, you don't have to be, sweetheart, because we're not, are we, kids?'

'No, Mam,' the two children chorused flatly. The boy glanced round at her anxiously before returning to the screen. Sarah patted the carpet and invited Nina to sit down.

'We're going to have loads of money now he's snuffed it but don't tell everyone or they'll all be round like vouchers,' she whispered loudly.

'Vultures, you daft 'nana!' the boy corrected.

'Yeah, when the insurance get their fingers out,' Mrs Boyle huffed. 'As long as the coroner says it wasn't suicide or we'll have nothing. Why they couldn't do the inquest straight away I don't know. Opening it then closing it again. It's obvious what happened. He fell in the river while he was out of his head. There was no note on him or anything, was there, Bonnie?'

'No,' Mrs Droy said immediately, 'there was no note.'

The 'cheerful' Mrs Boyle held out her glass, which was still half full, and smiled at Liam's dad. 'I'll have some more tonic water, Tone, if you've any going,' she cooed.

'Sure, sure,' Mr Droy said smoothly, fetching the plastic bottle and filling his guest's glass.

Mrs Boyle watched in silence as he poured the drink, then she turned to Dad, who'd just accepted a glass of whisky from Liam's mum, and told him she never touched anything stronger than orange juice, you know.

Dad shuffled uncomfortably next to me. 'Erm . . . no, I'm sure you don't—very understandable. Erm . . . it's a shame we've not had any snow for the kids, isn't it?' he began.

This was unbearable. 'Come on,' I said to Georgia, 'let's go show the boys how to take a thrashing.'

'Doesn't she care that her husband's dead?' Georgia asked as we sloped out.

'It's just the tablets she's taken,' I said guessing, 'but Thomas definitely cared about his dad, so don't say anything in here.'

'I won't. I'm not stupid.'

Liam was about to take a shot when we walked in. We must have distracted him because he made a real

130

pig's ear of it, missing the red completely and firing the white straight into a corner pocket. 'Thanks again, sucker!' Thomas said gleefully, retrieving the ball and placing it on the 'd'. Coolly, he bent to take his first shot. 'You'd think,' he said smugly, 'that when someone has their very own pool table to practise on day and night they'd be able to give you half a game, wouldn't you?'

'I guess,' I replied, puzzled by the icy undertones of his question.

Thomas jabbed the cue swiftly, sending his ball cleanly into the middle pocket. 'I guess,' he repeated, moving quickly to take his second shot.

I glanced at Liam, who smiled engagingly as if he hadn't a care in the world. 'Hi, gorgeous,' he said.

'Hi, ugly,' I replied.

'*I* was talking to Georgia,' he retorted, winking at my sister.

Her face flamed an immediate crimson. 'Hi, Liam,' she sighed. Had I taught her nothing all these years?

'Hey, Erin,' Thomas called, his voice almost a shout.

'Yeah?'

'Thanks for coming.'

'What do you mean?'

'To my dad's wake. Thanks for coming.'

'Em . . . when was it?' I asked, confused.

'When was it? It wasn't. Not allowed to bury the poor bastard yet, are we. Not until they've poked and prodded around until there's nothing left to poke and prod. So, we're going ahead without him, aren't we, to fit in with the festive season. Welcome to Tony and Bonnie's Rent-a-Party!' Liam scratched the side of his nose, staying resolutely silent. Thomas chalked his cue. 'You can rely on the Droys, you know, to solve all your problems. Have you got any problems, Erin? Cos Bonita and Tony and Liam, they'll sort them for you, just like that.' He blew a cloud of chalk dust into the air where it hung for a second as if, like me, it was unsure how it was expected to react.

I had known this was not going to be a comfortable event. After all, what do you say to someone whose father has just died? Thomas hadn't been to school since the news so I hadn't seen him to talk to but I had expected him to have been either subdued or, more typically, putting on a brave face; but sarcastic? Mr and Mrs Droy had done so much for them all since the tragedy, too. Obviously too much, from the sound of it.

Thomas bent to take another shot, revealing a tangle of empty bottles behind him. He'd been drinking then? That struck me as just a bit off, in the circumstances. 'Now, come on. Miss Mackiness, don't stand there with that sorrowful look on your posh little face because I know you've got problems.'

'Who hasn't?' I shrugged lightly.

'We've talked about them, haven't we?'

'Yes,' I admitted uncomfortably, 'we have.' I'd told him everything, starting with the table that night of the party, and later, during evenings of French homework, going on to my dad's bankruptcy and the savings. I'd

132

told him everything and he'd listened and understood and been kind. 'And you told me yours,' I reminded him.

'Yeah, but mine are all gone, now, aren't they? Mine are all six foot under.'

'Take it easy, guy. Not in front of the kids, eh?' Liam said, nodding towards Georgia.

I darted Liam a look of gratitude and tried to find safer ground. 'Speaking of problems,' I said hastily, 'Mr Whitehead's given us stacks of coursework to do over the holidays. I've written everything down for you if you want to see the stuff you missed when you were . . . away.'

Thomas's eyes narrowed scornfully. 'French? What use is that to someone like me? Or you, for that matter. You're one of us now, Erin, so don't go getting ideas above your station, lassie. It's leaving school at sixteen and straight to the checkouts for you. Isn't that right?'

Liam rescued me again, a wavering smile on his face, his voice full of admiration. 'No way! Erin's going to university, aren't you? It's all I ever hear from Mam. "Why don't you do more homework like Erin does? Erin's so bright. The school thinks Erin will get straight A stars. You could get an A star for art if you tried harder like Erin does, our Liam." Thanks for the pressure, blondie!'

'Well, you could!' I laughed. 'I've seen your portfolio—it's good.'

He groaned. 'Oh, she's never shown you all my stuff?'

'Every little doodle.'

'I like the ones of the girls with the big boobies,' Georgia piped up, not wanting to be outdone.

I thought between the three of us we had lightened the mood but Tommo shook his head and sneered. 'Nah, you're kidding yourself, Mackiness. Universities are more elitist now than when my dad went. Even if you start, you'll never see it through—no money, no degree. Barmaid, waitress, or checkouts, take your pick.'

My heart thudded as he threw my fears into my face. I tried again, hoping to distract him, telling myself it was part of the grieving process, this anger, this spite. 'Come on, Tom, you're really good at French; you have a natural flair for languages, Mr Whitehead says so.'

Thomas took a swig from one of the bottles behind him. 'Natural flair bollocks. It's money that talks, isn't it, Liam? You can be as thick as pig-shit but if you've got money that's all that matters, isn't it, pal? Isn't that what your dad told Riddick?' He glared hard at his best friend, challenging him to contradict.

Liam just shrugged, frowned at the green baize, then casually bent to take his shot. 'Whatever you say, mate,' he responded quietly, 'just keep the language down in front of the kid.'

I gazed at Liam, impressed. Ever since that night coming back from Stirling, my opinion of him had changed. There was more to him than the 'I'm the man' image I'd only seen before. Like now, the way he was handling Tommo, when Tommo was being so provocative and unfair. Liam caught my eye, and sent me a glimmer of a smile. I smiled back, hoping he would understand that I wanted to help him but I needed to get Georgia away before she protested that she wasn't a 'kid'. I couldn't risk Tommo turning on her, and in his state, there was no knowing what he'd say.

The atmosphere was becoming more and more tense, building sentence by sentence like it had that time in the classroom when Thomas had pricked Mrs Castle's hand, except this time, it seemed deliberate. Thomas wanted trouble.

I glanced at my watch, signalling to Georgia that it was time to escape. 'Got to go, lads, sorry,' I began.

'You haven't had a game yet,' Tommo spouted, 'stay for one game—doubles. Me and you take Liam and the sprog.'

Hastily, I turned down the invitation. 'I can't, sorry, I'm sleeping over at Katia's tonight—her parents are away so she's alone. I haven't even packed yet. See you at the disco on New Year, yeah?'

'Oh, coming slumming with us now are you?' Tommo asked menacingly.

'Pack it in, Tommo,' Liam said sharply, springing to my defence.

'Or what?'

'Just do it.'

I bundled Georgia through the door before I heard Tom's response.

* * *

'It was awful—really uncomfortable—he seemed set on causing trouble,' I told Katia that night as we struggled to get to sleep. 'I hope Liam was OK.'

'You sticking up for Liam—that's a first!'

'I know, but I felt sorry for him and for Thomas, I guess . . . I don't know . . . maybe I wouldn't deal with it any differently. I've only known one person who's died and that was my grandad but he'd been ill a long time and we expected it. And he was old.'

Katia 'mmd' sympathetically. 'You don't think they had a fight after you went, do you?' she asked.

'I don't think so. Liam's mum barged in with a plate of sausage rolls just as I dragged Georgia away, so don't worry. Lover Boy's face will be as beautiful as ever and your chance to snog him all night at the disco remains intact.'

It was her cue to lighten the conversation—which I wanted—but instead she let out a long, low fart from her futon and told me she wasn't that fussed about Master Droy any more.

'What?'

'I'm not!'

'Really?'

For some reason, I felt pleased by her revelation. I didn't believe it though. 'You're having me on, aren't you?'

'I'm not! Been there, done that. I'm ready for someone older, more mature, you know? Someone with his

136

own car like Chris Durham in Year Thirteen who happens to be the DJ on New Year's Eve.'

'So that's why you were making me walk round the sixth form block at the end of term. You weren't on a keep fit campaign at all!'

'Maybe, maybe not.'

I screwed my eyes up, trying to find her in the darkness. 'What does that mean, anyway? "Been there, done that"?'

'Shut up. Go to sleep.'

'Katia Maria Pulic?'

'Ernie Amy Mackiness?'

'Is there something you'd like to share with me?'

'Maybe, if you're ready to listen.'

'I'm all ears, as Gary Lineker said to Prince Charles.'

'Are you lying comfortably?'

'Indeed.'

'Then I'll begin. You know that night of the party?'

'Which party?'

'Mr Droy's.'

'Oh, that party. The uneventful one.'

'I had it with Liam.'

'Yeah, right, Kat. Course you did. Night-night—don't let the bedbugs bite.'

'No, seriously.'

'Kat, it's nearly three o'clock in the morning. I'm really, really tired.'

'And I'm really, really serious.'

I sighed heavily. 'I think I might have noticed something like that,' I said levelly.

137

'No you wouldn't, you were too busy hassling Mr Droy about your table, remember?'

'Let me get this straight. While I was humiliating myself in front of Mr Droy, you were having sex with his son?'

'Precisely.'

I rolled over towards her. 'You had sex with Liam?'

'Yep.'

'Real sex?'

'Yep.'

I lowered my voice, despite the fact there was no one to overhear. 'All the way?'

'Yep.'

'I don't believe you.'

'Why?' she asked, her voice hurt.

'Because there's absolutely no way you would have kept that to yourself for all this time. Not in a million years!' I hissed.

There was a long pause. I wanted her to tell me she was lying. For some reason, the thought of them together made my stomach shrivel. It wasn't jealousy—how could it be? It was just—well—it didn't seem right. He wouldn't do something like that—not with his mum and dad in the house.

'You'd think that, wouldn't you,' Katia grunted.

'What?' I said, startled that she had read my mind.

'You'd think it would have been impossible to keep that tasty news to myself, but you lot haven't been exactly receptive, have you? Gabriel's having extra tuition in this and extra tuition in that, you're always

138

moaning about having no money and how desperate you are to find a job . . . '

The job bit was true. Seven I'd applied for so far. I was either too young or too late or too inexperienced each time. 'Sorry for having an aim in life,' I responded curtly to the girl who didn't have a clue.

'Fine, you have your aims. So I try Hannah, but she's got her own thing going on.'

'That small thing of her mother thinking she had breast cancer, you mean.'

'Yeah, but she didn't in the end, did she?'

'She still had to have a lump removed. It wasn't nice.' Katia was annoying me now, with her glib, superficial answer to everything.

'Did I say it was? All I'm saying is I was waiting for the right moment, once Hannah had calmed down, and Gabriel was allowed out of the house, and you stopped having aims, to break my news, when what happens?'

'What?'

'Thomas Boyle's dad tops himself!'

'There was no note,' I informed her brusquely. Some of us cared.

'Whatever. All I know is my trivial little event couldn't compete with any of that stuff, so that's why, in a nutshell, I didn't tell you. Do you want to know the details?'

'No I don't! Not after a supper of Pop Tarts and cocoa!' I twisted hastily away, my face so close to the wall my nose pressed into the wallpaper. I did not want to hear any details. I did not want those images in my mind.

We didn't speak for ages. I could hear the clock ticking nearby and Katia's breathing. After a few minutes, she tugged my nightshirt. 'Shall I really tell you why I kept it quiet?' she whispered.

'If you must.'

'It was awful.'

I was taken aback, not by her words, but by the catch in Katia's voice that she always had when she was close to tears. 'Awful?' I asked.

'I mean, I thought it was great at first, when I was climbing up the steps to his bedroom. I remember thinking to myself, "You've done it, Kat, you clever girl, your dream is about to come true," even if he did seem in a huff because I'd told him you thought he was a slime-ball, I was actually going to his bedroom. Me!'

'What did you tell him I thought he was a slime-ball for?' I snapped.

'Just listen, will you? It's difficult enough explaining.'

'Sorry.'

' . . . it wasn't dreamy at all. He just . . . he just wanted to get it over with, I think. He didn't kiss me or anything just . . . it hurt a bit, too—so all that rubbish about horse riding breaking you in is a total myth—and in the end it was just quick and sticky and . . . empty. Mum says . . . '

'Mum says? You have never discussed it with your mum?'

140

'Well, who better to discuss it with? You're so narrow-minded sometimes, Ernie,' Katia retorted irritably.

'I am not.'

'Let me finish, please, Erin. I really need to share this with you.'

'OK, sorry.'

'When I told Mum, she was as miserable as I was.'

'Because of you being under-age?'

'No! My mum lives in the real world—she knows if it's going to happen it's going to happen whatever the law says and she was proud that I'd used a condom but . . . she says what she forgot to tell me was that no matter how much you fancy a person, sex is crap if they don't fancy you back.'

I would have thought that was obvious but didn't say anything. Katia was still finding it difficult to keep her voice under control. 'And he clearly didn't fancy me. I was just another notch on his bed-post, wasn't I? Afterwards,' she wavered, 'I pretended everything was cool—you know—smiling and being casual. I had to—I mean, I was the one who'd done all the running. I was behaving like I thought Liam expected—you know—like I say, I presumed I was just another conquest but . . . you're going to laugh at this . . . '

'What?'

'He was upset.'

'Upset?'

'Yeah—the great stud Liam Droy. When he got dressed he was stammering and he could hardly get his legs in his trousers and he hadn't had *that* much to drink.

141

Well, anyway, I went right off him after that. I can't look at him now. You won't tell anyone, will you? I don't want Hannah and Gabriel giving me grief about it.'

'I promise,' I said.

'Thanks. You don't mind, do you?'

'What?'

'About what happened?'

'No, why should I? It's your body.'

'I know, it's just that you and Liam seem a lot friend-lier these days . . . I sometimes wonder.'

'Nah! It's only because we live near each other. He's still a moron,' I said quickly.

'For once I agree with you,' she sighed. We lay in silence again, lost in thought, until Katia eventually fell asleep, her soft snores rhythmic and soothing.

I lay awake much longer, running through every-thing Katia had told me. I wasn't surprised, really, that she'd had sex. Katia was always going to be the first out of her, Hannah, and me—she had always done everything first, from shaving her legs to kissing with tongues. Yes, she was always going to be first. I just wish it hadn't been with Liam.

Not the Liam I knew now, anyway. The old Look-at-me-Liam—fine—she was welcome to him, but the new Liam—the one who stuck up for me and yet stayed loyal to his friends. The one who teased my sis-ters and hung back for me every morning, happy just to walk in silence next to me. The one who looked at me with such depth of emotion sometimes. I wish it hadn't been that Liam.

14

I spent the next morning looking round the sales with Katia and Hannah, trying not to think about her revelation as we fought our way through the shops in the trendy Queen's Arcade.

Katia's subdued mood from last night had been completely replaced by the joy of shopping. She was one of those people who didn't beat herself up if she made a mistake—she just got on with making the next one and I loved her for it. I knew in a few months' time her memory of what had happened with Liam would be totally different from the account she had shared with me last night. But I didn't want to dwell on it, either. Instead I followed her and Hannah to the checkouts where Katia was about to buy yet another item of clothing she just had to have.

As we neared the front of the queue, there was a chorus of irritated muttering from customers as the girl on the counter, harassed and under pressure, made a mess of inserting a new till roll into the machine. I remembered what Thomas had said in the pool room and stared at the red-faced girl thinking, is that me in two years' time?

I had always taken it for granted that I would go to university. What if I couldn't go now, no matter how well I did in my exams, just because we had no money? I wanted to work in Paris. I wanted to drink coffee at pavement cafés wearing chic suits and looking enigmatic. I wanted to live in a flash apartment with a wrought-iron balcony overlooking a tree-lined avenue. I did not want to be a checkout girl. But what if Thomas was right? What if I had no choice? Both Mum and Dad had been to college and look at them now. Even Thomas's dad, Benny, had been to college and look at *him* now.

As we traipsed into yet another steeply-priced clothes shop, I began to feel more and more excluded. I watched as Katia held a low cut top against Hannah and encouraged her to buy it for the New Year disco. I smiled brightly, pretending I didn't mind I couldn't buy one, too. Any spare cash I had went towards my spending money for the trip which I was determined I would provide. That money thing again.

'Look at that neckline. My mum won't let me out in that!' Hannah protested.

'Oh go on,' Katia begged, 'it's not as if you're filling it with melons, is it, Han? We're talking garden peas, let's be honest!'

'Charming!' Hannah laughed, twisting round to show the top to me. 'What do you think, Erin? Do you dare me to buy it?'

'Always do dares,' I advised.

144

'What about you? Are you going to get one? I'll treat you if you like.'

She would, too, without a second thought, but her offer stung because I couldn't reciprocate. 'No, I'm sorted, thanks. I got something new at Christmas,' I lied.

'Did you? What?' Katia immediately asked.

'Hey,' I said, glancing in shock-horror-surprise at my watch, 'we're supposed to have met Gabriel in Waterstone's five minutes ago—look at the length of that queue. Come on!'

'Since when has Gabriel been on time for anything?' Hannah asked, nevertheless threading her way between displays of reduced items that were supposedly so, so cheap but still so, so expensive if you didn't have enough. As I followed them to the counter, I thought about Thomas and how he must have felt like this a million times when he was out with Liam and understood a little bit of his bitterness towards the Droys. Full of good intentions as they were, and Hannah had just been, charity was the last thing you wanted.

Gabriel was on his second pot of tea by the time we arrived in the bookshop's coffee bar. 'Where've you lot been?' he complained. 'It's been murder keeping this table free!'

We slapped our cold hands against his cheeks a few times, threw his bags on the floor and told him we were sorry. 'Says you, anyway! I've waited hours for you in the past!' Hannah reminded him.

'I was early because I have news!' he said eagerly, leaning forward and almost elbowing his teapot onto the floor.

'Steady, boy!' I said.

His cheeks, already pink from our gentle greeting, flushed deeper, the colour spreading to his neck where it clashed nastily with his orange *I see dead people* T-shirt. We told him to get on with it before Katia came with the coffees or he would never get a word in.

'No, I want Kat here, too. This news is momentous!' he grinned.

We had to wait until Katia had delivered the drinks, returned the tray, explained to us that the weird-looking things on the plate in the middle were called biscotti, yes, they did taste as foul as they looked but they were trendy and expensive, so shut up.

'I have news!' Gabriel interrupted, rocking the edge of the table so that all the crockery shook.

'Is it momentous?' Hannah asked.

'Spill,' ordered Katia.

Gabriel leaned back, the grin splitting his face like an enormous pistachio shell. 'I, Gabriel Owens aged fourteen of The Vicarage, North Carlton, wish to announce to all those gathered here today that I . . . girls, a drum roll, please.'

We obliged and I'm sure no one in the café was annoyed at the deafening sound at all, much.

'I am a boyfriend!' Gabriel announced and immediately launched into minute detail about how the woman who had been giving him extra maths and

146

English lessons had a daughter, Jessica, at private school and she'd come home for the holidays and she had watched him bent over his *Macbeth* in her living room and they'd got chatting and one thing had led to another and he'd asked her out and she'd said yes and that was it, he was in love.

'Jessica,' Katia said, chewing thoughtfully on her biscotti.

'Yes, Jessica,' Gabriel said dreamily.

Katia squinted her eyes. 'You do know that if she hurts you, we'll have to kill her?'

'Seems fair to me,' Gabriel agreed amiably.

'Are you bringing her to the disco on New Year's Eve?' I asked.

He bit his lip apologetically and said he'd been invited to Jessica's for a firework supper. Several jokes about eating fireworks later, Hannah confessed that she wasn't coming, either. 'But you've just bought that top!' Katia pointed out.

'I know, I know, I just . . . I want to see the New Year in with my mum, you know, after all she's been through. Sophie's staying at Dad's so she'll be on her own.'

'She could always come round to my house and watch Jools Holland with my lot,' I said, disappointed. I knew Hannah hadn't been out in ages and I had been looking forward to having a good natter with her.

'Well, it's not only that,' Hannah faltered, glancing at me briefly before fixing her gaze on the biscotti, 'Mum's worried about the . . . er . . . area—she feels

147

it might be a bit risky round there at that time of night. The car got scratched, you know, last time we parked outside your house and that was daytime.'

'Did it? Ours never has been,' I said in a small voice. I felt as if I had been punched in the stomach. One of my closest friends scared to visit me. How bad was that?

'Your mum fusses too much,' Katia declared.

'Your mum doesn't fuss enough,' Hannah fired instantly back.

'And my mum's going to kill me if I'm not home in time to babysit!' I announced. Hastily I scraped my chair back and gathered my things before someone said something they would regret.

'I didn't know you were babysitting,' Katia called after me. I responded with a quick wave and disappeared through the Mind and Spirit section. I just wanted to be alone. Outside, it had begun to drizzle again. I pulled up the collar on my coat and headed towards the bus station.

'You're back early,' Mum smiled as I flounced in. 'Tea's just poured, if you'd like some.'

'I just want to be alone,' I said brusquely. 'I'm going upstairs.'

Mum tipped a pile of digestives onto a plate and informed me that Georgia was upstairs with Megan. 'They're doing strange girlie things with cotton wool balls and nail varnish, according to Nina.'

'Oh, what? I just wanted some space for once!' I snapped.

'It's Georgia's bedroom too,' Mum pointed out, heading into the front room. No, really?

I sank on to the kitchen chair, staring at the kitchen table. It was already stained and dinted, its cheap wood unable to take the punishments of family life no matter how many place mats we guarded it with. I hated it. Tears filled my eyes. I could feel them bulging heavily in each lower eyelid until they overflowed down my face. They came stealthily at first, like prisoners escaping from jail; large ringleader-tears spearheading the break, followed by the hangers-on carving a salty trail. I tried to brush them away but they kept on coming until I just gave up and sank my head into my arms and cried and cried.

Of course, Mum and Dad came charging in. You can't have a decent sobbing session in a small house. I felt Mum's arms around my shoulder and sensed Dad's concerned presence. 'Erin, love, what's wrong? What's happened?' Mum asked, panic in her voice.

I managed a routine 'Nothing, leave me alone.'

No chance. Mum's voice got higher and higher. 'Have you been hurt? Has someone hurt you?'

'Mum! Stop asking "mum" questions! I'm just fed up, that's all.'

'Let me talk to her,' Dad said soothingly. 'Erin, what's wrong?'

I said the first thing that came into my head. 'I just want the table back,' I stuttered.

'The table's gone.'

'I don't want it to be gone. I want it back.'

'I thought we'd dealt with the table,' Mum added, puzzled.

But Dad was in psychologist mode. 'It's not just about the table, is it, Erin? Come on, tell us what's really bothering you. Here.'

A cotton handkerchief was stuffed into the crook of my arms. My fingers scrabbled for it gratefully because I had reached the snotty stage by now. I lifted my head slightly and blew. 'Thanks,' I snorted.

'No problem,' Dad said.

I heard a chair being pulled back and knew he was next to me. It was comforting, having him so close, knowing he would listen and wanted to help. 'I don't want to be a checkout girl, either,' I stammered, 'or leave school at sixteen like the Scrunchies.'

'A checkout girl?' Mum repeated.

'What do you mean, Erin?' Dad prompted.

What did I mean? I wasn't sure myself but I took a deep breath and out they gushed, all my hiccuppy, pathetic thoughts and emotions. 'Well . . . like . . . you know—now that we live here and we're poor I won't be able to go to university because I'll have to earn my keep and bring a wage into the house and spend every Boxing Day with people on anti-depressants and Hannah's mum won't let her come to the Centre because we live in a no-go area and it's only a matter of time before Katia dumps me too because she's more mature than me and does things I

150

don't do yet and that'll only leave Gabriel who'll stick with me because he has to because he's a Christian but even Gabriel's got a girlfriend now called Jessica and I don't feel I belong anywhere because I'm too posh for The Close but too trashy to go shopping in the Queen's Arcade . . . '

'Whoa! Whoa! One thing at a time, Erin, one thing at a time,' Dad protested; which is a good job because I was about to add 'and I'm confused about Liam'.

'The table,' Mum said, 'start with the table.'

I started with the table. 'Well, after you sold it, I wrote to Mr Droy . . . '

'You wrote to Tony?'

'Yes,' I muttered, 'I wrote to him to ask him to reserve it for me, until I'd saved up to buy it back— that's why I've been trying to get a Saturday job, not just for the trip—but for the table, as a surprise—but when I asked him about it at his party, he said he never received my letter and he'd already sold it. I told him I don't see how he couldn't have got the letter when I delivered it myself by hand . . . '

'He can't read, love,' Mum said gently.

'What?' I sniffed from somewhere in my cocoon.

'Tony can't read; he's illiterate. He'll have put your letter in the bin, darling.'

'Well, that was a waste of flaming time then, wasn't it?' I said gruffly, glancing at Mum out of the corner of my eye.

Mum smiled. 'Yes, it was a bit.'

'How can he not read? He runs a massive business.'

'He's developed coping strategies over the years. It's quite clever, really, isn't it, Noel? Bonita was telling us.'

Dad nodded and agreed Tony had done remarkably well for himself, in the circumstances. Then Mum made me promise not to mention it to anyone because Mr Droy would be mortified if people found out.

'I don't know why everyone's fixated with that damned table anyway,' Dad said, 'huge, pretentious thing bruising your shins every time you sat down. We should have left it in The Lodge in the first place—the Colemans would have bought it—huge, pretentious couple that they were.'

'Oh,' Mum said at this unexpected revelation about the people who had bought our house, 'you've never told me that before.'

'How could I? It was your "heirloom",' Dad replied wiping his hand theatrically across his forehead. 'Oh, my table, it's Victorian, you know! Oh! Oh!'

Instead of being offended, Mum laughed and shook her head, 'OK! OK! Maybe I was a bit precious about it but . . . Erin, Erin, look at me.'

I struggled upright, slightly startled to find both of them so close to me, giving me their full attention. Now that I had stopped blubbering, they both seemed a little more relaxed. Mum, especially, looked quite— I don't know—pretty. 'Erin,' she said, clamping her hand over mine, 'the most important thing to us in this world is our children's happiness and future. We chose to sell that table to pay for your trip to France; it was a valid means to a valid end. There's no point filling yourself with regrets—life's too short.'

'That's just a cliché.'

'Come on! I'd known that table longer than you. If I can get over it, so can you.'

'But what about when it's Georgia's turn and Nina's to go on trips and we run out of things to sell?' I asked.

'We won't,' Dad said firmly. 'We're sorting the money out, bit by bit. Look, Erin, I messed up once. I didn't listen to my instincts with Steve Rawlinson and I've paid for it. That was my big mistake in life but I'm dealing with it. So what are you saying? That because I messed up, your life is over? You're doomed to be a checkout girl and so is Georgia and so is Nina? Rubbish!'

'The family next door to Bonnie's have two children at university,' Mum added, 'and they were born and bred on the estate.'

Back to Dad. The pair of them were making my head reel. 'OK, it is going to be that bit harder for you when you do go to university than if we hadn't lost the business; you will have to work your way through, maybe even as a checkout girl, but you will be going. There's no doubt about it.'

'How can you be so sure?' I asked, unconvinced.

'Because we sold the table!' Dad laughed.

'I don't get you,' I said.

Mum squeezed my hand. 'It shows we'll help you any way we can, even if we have to sell special things.'

'But,' Dad added heavily, 'we can only do so much— in the end it's up to you. But if you use this house as an excuse for everything that goes wrong in your life you're not the girl I thought you were.'

'I'm not making excuses, I'm just confused!' I protested.

Dad kissed me on the head and said gently, 'No, Erin, this isn't confusing, this is easy. Out there is confusing—in here is home.'

I knew he was right. I knew I didn't have to deal with dead parents, divorced parents, or even darling-tell-me-everything-I'm-your-best-friend parents. Just loving strapped-for-cash parents. I'd try and remember that next time I was in the Queen's Arcade. 'I know,' I said, my voice small and cracked, 'I'm being a pain in the bum, aren't I?'

They both agreed instantly. 'Now can I watch the end of the rugby?' Dad asked.

'Yes,' I consented.

'Keep the hanky,' he added as I blew away the last of my uncertainties.

'Now,' Mum said, edging closer, 'about Katia.'

'Erm.'

Mum raised her eyebrows and I knew what was next. Something along the lines of 'What did you mean by more mature and does it involve boys? If so, what sort of boys?' So predictable. So Mum, my caring, brilliant mother. It was then that I realized why she was looking so pretty. 'Mum!' I said, throwing my arms round her.

'What? What?' she gasped, I like to think in a delighted, not squashed, kind of way.

154

'You've had your roots done!'

She touched her hair and smiled. 'Yeah, this morning. What do you think?'

'I think I'm beginning to feel normal.'

I headed upstairs, ready to dump my overnight stuff. The bedroom door was slightly ajar, so I peered in first, out of curiosity. Nina and Megan the Wonderbra were leaning against the wall on Georgia's side, a look of awe on their faces. I couldn't see Georgia but I could hear her. 'This is another good one,' she said, 'listen to this. "I'm nineteen and six months ago my ex-boyfriend gave me . . . " '

I coughed loudly and the recital stopped pronto. 'Hi, guys,' I said, breezily, 'mind if I come in?'

'Er, no,' Georgia stammered innocently.

I grinned reassuringly at her and tossed my bag behind her so that we could all pretend I hadn't seen my magazine stuffed under her backside. 'OK?' I asked her.

'Yes. We were just . . . hanging out. I suppose we all have to go now, don't we?' she asked sulkily.

'No, why should you? It's your bedroom as much as mine.'

Did those words really just fly out of my mouth? Oh, well, too late now. A look of confusion followed swiftly by total disbelief flittered across my sister's face. She stared at me, as if waiting for the punchline. Was I such a control freak? 'Do you mind if I stay, though? I want to decorate,' I asked politely.

'Decorate?'

'Dad said they were decorating my bedroom first,' Nina wailed. 'I'm having jungle wallpaper and that green snake from Ikea when they've saved up two months' child benefit.'

'I know, I know, that's why Georgia and me need to have something in between times, don't we, sis?'

'I guess. Erin?'

'What?'

'Have you been drinking?'

'No. Why?'

'Your eyes are all red and you're being nice.'

'Tch! Can't I be friendly without people thinking I'm drunk?'

'No!' the three of them chorused.

'*Merde!*'

I hunted round the drawers in my desk until I found my hidden cache of 'stuff'. 'Anyone want to help?' I asked, brandishing my brand-new marker pens Santa had left for me.

'What do we do?' Georgia asked.

'Watch and learn, sister,' I instructed, clambering onto the bed and facing the wall. I stood for a second, contemplating who to go for first, then with a joyous 'pop' as the top came off, I homed in on the number nine and gave him a purple affro.

'You're drawing on the wallpaper!' Nina cried out in astonishment. 'That is so naughty!'

'I know,' I grinned, 'naughty but nice.'

156

15
LIAM

I'm just wondering whether to catch another half hour's kip when I hear the mechanical whirring of the garage door opening beneath my bedroom and that solves that one. Dad gets a bit narked if I'm not up before he's back from work. It's only just gone two in the afternoon, mind, so he's early, but I remember it's Saturday and that explains it.

He gives me a right dead-eye when I come down and ask Mam what's for breakfast. 'Breakfast? Breakfast at this time? You've got a nerve, lad,' he grumbles.

As he slackens off his tie and tells me how many hours he's already put in at the shops I yawn and stretch, just to annoy him. Dad threatens to clobber me if I don't stop playing the wise-guy.

'Oh, leave the lad alone,' Mum says as she slots bread into the toaster, 'he needs his sleep.'

'For what?' Dad asks. 'Because it certainly isn't doing his looks any good.'

'Ha-ha, Dad, hilarious! Don't give up the day job will you?' I tell him.

Bad move. I always forget he needs at least five fags and a bucket of coffee before he's fit to talk to after work. He's down on me like a ton of bricks. 'Look, Liam,' he says, cocking his thumb at Mam, 'you're going to have to learn to cut the apron strings, because once you leave that school you'll wonder what's hit you—you'll be starting at eight like the rest of us and coming home at eight like the rest of us.'

'I know, I know. Don't get a cob on. I'll pull my weight.'

'Damned right you will because there'll be no favouritism.'

'No favouritism. Got it.'

'And no attitude.'

'No favouritism, no attitude. Got it.'

Mam slides a plate of beans on toast in front of me and a mug of coffee in front of Dad. 'Honestly, Tony, you'll frighten him to death. You'll have him not wanting to work for you the way you go on.'

Dad laughs at her and snorts, 'Oh, aye, what else is he going to do?'

Mam sticks her nose in the air and goes, 'I don't know. He might want to go to art college or something for all we know.'

'Art college?' Dad stares at her, stares at me, then stares back at her, before cracking up. 'Ah, thanks,' he says, taking a deep sip of his coffee, 'I do like a joke after a hard day.'

I stare at Mam as well because I don't know where she's got that idea from. I've never thought about going to art college or any other college in my life. That'll be Mrs Mack putting ideas into her head again. Mam's always coming out with wild notions about education these days, but there's no way I'm staying on at school a minute longer than I have to. She's about to say something else when the phone rings and she goes to get it.

I offer to get Dad another coffee and he nods and says thanks. 'I'm sorry if I come across as a bit heavy, son,' he says, 'but you will have to sharpen up when you get in the workshops. You'll be under a lot of pressure being the gaffer's son. You'll have to learn to be an outsider, not quite one of the lads, and that's hard.'

'I can take it. Anyway, I've got another year at school to go yet. If I can stick that, I can stick anything.'

He peers at me through a haze of smoke and nods again. Dad totally knows where I'm at. He's a great geezer and one day, I'll tell him so. Mam comes in, one hand over the receiver, and asks if I've seen Tommo.

'How have I? I've just got up.'

'Well, do you know where he might be? He never went home after his paper round this morning and Gayle's worried.'

I shake my head. Last time I saw him was four days ago. Boxing Day, and we didn't exactly part on brilliant terms. I mean, the guy's suffering, right, and he's got to let it go somewhere but when I'd told him he was out of order with Erin and Georgia he'd said 'screw you' and left. I haven't spoken to him since but I know he'll be round when he's ready. It's no big deal.

Mum tells Mrs B I don't know anything and makes her promise to call when she hears from him. 'That poor woman—as if she hasn't got enough on her plate,' Mam says after she's hung up.

That 'poor woman' is afraid of her own shadow these days and won't leave the house unless Mam ferries her somewhere. According to Mam, Benny's death has finally hit home and she's now full of guilt and remorse and wishing she could turn the clock back. The sooner the doctor sets up counselling for Mrs B the better. Still, she should put more trust in Tommo. I know he won't have gone far—he's just having time out somewhere. I thank Mam for the nosh and try to escape but she points to the glass dish on the worktop and asks me to take it over to Sue's.

'What?'

'Take the trifle dish back to Sue's and say thank you,' she repeats slowly.

'Do I have to?'

'What's up?' Dad asks. 'Is it too heavy for you?'

'Funny guy.'

I grab the dish and get instant earache about not dropping it.

The Espace is missing so I figure they're out. I knock a couple of times just in case then head straight back down the path. I just reach the gate, which is crying out for a lick of Hammerite, when Erin calls my name. I twist round and I do almost drop the 'kin' dish because she's standing there with a towel wrapped round her head and just these baggy jogging bottoms on and a short sports top that shows her midriff and she looks fantastic. 'Brought this,' I mumble.

'Oh, great, thanks. Come in.'

'I . . . er . . . '

She's already gone inside, leaving the door open, so I follow. I feel so weak, man.

In the kitchen she's unwrapped the towel and is rubbing her hair roughly. She's got this big grin on her face and a look I can't figure. I want to speak but my mouth feels as if it's full of polystyrene and I just hold out the bowl and pray she'll take it off me quick. Instead she nods to the sink and tells me to put it on the draining board.

She grins and does this funny wriggly thing with her eyebrows that makes me want to laugh and throw up at the same time. Then she tells me to put the kettle on and chucks out instructions about where to find the coffee and there's sugar in the cupboard if I need it while she plugs in the hairdryer and starts drying her hair. 'Don't tell my mum I'm drying it in here—she's got this hygiene thing about hair and kitchens but it's freezing upstairs.'

'Mine's the same,' I fib.

'So, what's new?'

I try to think of something impressive but then she suddenly drops her head so that her hair tumbles forward and I can see her vertebrae sticking out like a row of perfect, white mints and I can hardly breathe.

'Not much milk in mine,' she says.

'What?'

161

'Trainers.'

'What?'

She looks up at me and makes herself go cross-eyed. 'Duh! My coffee, Liam.'

'Oh.'

'What are you trying to do? Hypnotize the kettle into boiling?'

I jump to it and start shovelling coffee into mugs and crack on I know what I'm doing. 'Where is everyone?' I ask.

She lets out this grunt. 'Picking Grandma up from the station. She's decided to see the New Year in with us.'

'That'll be nice though, having your gran over.'

'You don't know my grandma, do you?'

'No. Is she hard work?'

Erin hunches her shoulders. 'No, not really—not with me anyway—she just has this knack of saying the wrong thing at the wrong time. Like when Mum told her she'd have more space at one of the hotels in town, she said "Oh, don't worry, sleeping in a council house will be like appearing on *Lifeswaps*."'

'I thought you were on that once. On the bus when you first moved here—do you remember?'

'I remember. You said me living here was like the queen moving to Coronation Street.'

'Yeah, I did.'

'God, I hated it here at first.'

'You made that obvious enough,' I told her.

'I know. I wasn't very subtle about it, was I? I thought moving to a council estate was the worst

162

thing that could happen to someone. How dumb can you get?'

Erin switches the hairdryer off and pulls out the plug. She ruffles through her hair briskly, all the time chatting to me as if we did this every day. We touch on Boxing Day but don't dwell on Tommo's behaviour. It's as if we both understand he was a prat but we both also understand why. 'Hey,' she continues, 'have you heard about my mum's latest venture? She's applied for a special licence to use the Espace as a taxi. She says it has to earn its keep along with the rest of us! She wants to use it mainly to take girls home after school discos and stuff. I think it's a great idea, don't you?'

I nod, overwhelmed by the huge smile she gives me as I hand her the coffee. Now you wouldn't give a smile like that to someone you thought was a slime-ball, would you? I smile back, thinking, this is nice. Having a little chat with your neighbour. What a pleasant way to spend a Saturday afternoon in the middle of winter. I do not think, God, Erin, you are hotter than lava. Not at all, at all. 'Grandma thinks it's outrageous, of course. *"A taxi driver? Are you mad, Susan?"* I'm just glad I've got the disco to escape to tomorrow night.'

'Yeah—it should be good. They've got Stiff PK doing the dee-jaying—he's amazing,' I tell her.

'I thought Chris Durham was doing it?'

'That ponce? No chance!'

'Katia'll be disappointed.'

She looks at me strangely, as if she's testing my reaction. 'Oh,' is the best I can come up with.

163

I glance round for somewhere to put my coffee, thinking, time to go, buddy. That little episode last month is still haunting me and if I wasn't such a strong character I reckon I'd need counselling for stress, never mind Mrs B. Even the mention of Katia's name makes me shudder.

Then Erin comes right out with it. No messing about the bush. 'She told me, you know, about what happened.' There's a pause where she sees the look on my face and she adds, 'I hope you don't mind.'

'Why should I mind?' I bluff. 'Anyway, I'm surprised she can remember anything she was so out of it.'

Erin nods sadly. 'I know. I've told her she needs to be careful next time.'

I feel uncomfortable. What have they been doing—dissecting every move I made? 'Well, the slag won't be having a next time with me, and you can tell her that when you see her!' I say angrily.

Erin's face clouds over and I know I'm in for a nagging session. I always forget how prickly she is about her mates. Chantal blows hot and cold with hers all the time, slagging them off one minute, arm-in-arm the next. Erin would never do that. Her eyes sharpen and I glance round, thinking maybe her gran will come in and rescue me.

'There's no need to be so defensive, Liam. She doesn't want a "next time" with you, either, and don't call her a slag. You were there, too, remember—what does that make you?'

It's all going wrong. It started off so good but now

it is all going wrong. I was back to being a slime-ball and she's back to Ice-Queen, but I'm not backing down on this one. 'I'm just saying,' I say, edging towards the door, 'I mean, she wasn't exactly a virgin, was she?'

'Yes!' Erin says calmly. 'That's exactly what she was.'

'What?'

'It's true!'

'You're joking?'

'Why would I joke about it?'

'I was first? You're sure? You're not doing one of those girl-trick-things?'

Erin tuts. 'I don't do "girl-trick-things" thank you very much for confusing me with an airhead!'

'Wow!' I sigh and sit down.

'It was your first time, too, wasn't it?' Erin asks quietly.

I shrug. 'Maybe. What's wrong with that?'

'Nothing. Nothing at all.'

'Who else knows?' I ask.

'Just me and her mum as far as I know.'

'Her mum? Oh, Christ. You won't tell mine, will you? Mam and Dad'll kill me if they find out.'

'I know they will! I've heard your mum going on.'

'And on and on.' I catch Erin's eye, comforted that she understands about my family. I begin to feel less stressed about the Katia thing. It doesn't seem such a big deal now with her having been a virgin, too. I can put it down to my one mistake Dad had said everyone was entitled to. I tell Erin I'm sorry. 'I was out of order, calling Katia that.'

'Apology accepted. How do you . . . er . . . feel about her now?'

'Feel?'

'Does it change things now you know you were first?'

'What do you mean?'

'It's special, isn't it? The two of you? It would be for me, anyway. I can ask Katia for you, if you want to see her again . . . maybe tomorrow night?'

'No!' I shout. 'No way—I mean—she's all right—a bit fa—' I stop myself in time and Erin shakes her head at me as if I'm a lost cause. 'No, thanks. It wasn't that special . . . but, yeah, it should have been—it would have been if it had been with—No, don't say anything to her, please.'

Erin glances at me briefly, a frown on her face, but she doesn't say anything. Neither of us speaks for a bit. She scratches at something on her joggers and I go into one of those trances, like when you're having your hair cut and you just totally relax. Then we both look up at the same time and our eyes meet. My heart feels as if it's doing a high-five with my lungs as she smiles at me. 'Dance with me tomorrow night at the disco,' I blurt out.

'What?'

My mouth's as dry as astro-turf as I repeat the question. 'Dance with me tomorrow night—just once—please.'

'OK,' she agrees, 'just once.'

166

16

I walk home ecstatic. I go straight upstairs and plan the big moment. I lie on my bed thinking how much it would help if I could actually dance. If a slow one comes on, I'll be all right. I can smooch. What was that one she liked at Dad's fortieth? That old All Saints one? I rack my brain, trying to remember. We had it somewhere on a compilation—Mam used to 'dancercise' in turquoise lycra to it. Anyway, whatever it was, I'll get Stiff to play it. As soon as it comes on, I'll go up to Erin and take her hand and . . . I close my eyes, imagining the scene but just as I wrap my arms around her (she's wearing her hair up again and that black dress) the phone rings next to my bed. 'Lovely Linda's massage parlour—how can I help you?' I say.

'Liam—Tommo.'

'Tommo! Long time no hear, bud.'

'Things to sort out.'

He sounds fine. No edge to his voice. No slurring. I risk having a dig. 'I hear you went AWOL with the *Daily Mirrors*. Where are you?'

'McDonald's.'

'Fine choice! Get me a Big Mac meal in and I'll be there in ten.'

'I don't think you will, somehow, unless you're coming by rocket. I'm in Stirling.'

'You are kidding?'

'Nope.'

'When are you coming back?' I ask.

'When I've sorted *the things* out. Tell me where you sat, first off.'

'What?'

'You and Dad—where did you sit when you were here with him?'

'I dunno—near that plant thing.'

His voice fades in and out as he walks towards the table. 'Right,' he says.

'What are you doing up there, Tommo? It's miles away. You'll never make it for the evening round.'

He doesn't react for ages and when he does, his voice is still level but his words explode around me like long-planted landmines. 'The thing I hate about you most, Droy, is that you were the last of us to see him.'

'What?'

'Not me, not our James or Sarah, but you and that really gets me. You didn't even like him. You thought he was trash. Go on, admit it,' Tommo spits, 'admit you thought my dad was trash.'

There was no bottling out of this one. Whatever I did, the landmines were going to blow my legs off anyway, so I go for honesty. It's the only way with someone who reads you like a book. 'OK, I admit it. I thought he was a loser. I thought he should have tried harder to quit drinking when he had three kids to support but he . . . he loved you, so I respect him for that.'

Tommo goes quiet then whispers sarcastically, 'That's not like you, Droy, saying the "L" word. Not going gay on me, are you?'

'Well, that's what he told me, you wanted the truth, you got the truth.'

Tommo's voice cracks then. 'Are you being serious?' he asks.

And I know, for once in my thick life, that I've hit something so raw that whatever I say next matters, it really matters. I repeat the last conversation I had with Benny, almost word for word. And as I listen to myself, I realize what a blind, selfish git I've been. All this time, I've been presuming Tommo should feel the same way I do, cos we're best mates, right? And best mates think alike, don't they? Not once have I stopped to think how I'd feel if it was the other way round, and it had been my dad who'd died. Christ, if it had been my dad they'd fished up like a bloated inner tube out of that water I'd go insane.

Slowly, I repeat Benny's last words but I don't tell Tommo he was crying when he said them and I don't tell Tommo how relieved I was to see the back of him. For once, I say the right thing. 'I'm sorry, Tommo, I should have told you sooner, I'm sorry.'

There is no sound coming from the other end and I wonder if he's still there. I blather on, having to stop to clear my throat all the time because I'm choked. 'You're absolutely spot on, Tommo, it should have been you with Benny and not me but you were trying to sort your mam out. It's not your fault you weren't there for him.'

Tommo eventually sighs down the receiver. 'Yeah—that's the story of my life—running from one to the other trying to sort them out.'

'It's like they say, life's a bitch then you die.'

I hear a laugh then, and I relax slightly.

'Such comforting words, mate,' he sniffs.

'Yeah, well, we haven't all got your flair for languages.'

There's another pause before Tommo speaks again. 'He would have died anyway, you know. The first autopsy report showed his liver was riddled. Cirrhosis. He didn't have to fall in a chuffing river to die. He could have died in his own bed and I could have nursed him.'

There he went again—blaming himself for something that wasn't his fault. 'Tommo, come home, mate. Your mam's worried.'

'Yeah, I know. I should have told her what I was doing but it was just spur of the moment, you know? I had the urge to come back here.'

'Course you did. I'd have done the same.'

'Would you?'

'Yeah. Definitely. To feel closer to him, like.'

There's another pause. 'I'm sorry, mate, if I've been a bit harsh, it's just sometimes you and your family are a bit . . . '

I fill in the word for him. 'Interfering.'

'Something like that. I appreciate what you've done and everything but I always feel I owe you all the time.'

He says this with such sorrow in his voice I put him out of his misery straight away. 'You don't owe us anything, Tommo, but I hear what you're saying. Just come home safe, mate. I'll see you tomorrow at the Centre. And Tommo?'

'Aye?'

'Wear something decent for once, mate.'

He laughs and tells me to eff off.

Half an hour later Gayle calls and tells us Tommo's safe and in Stirling of all places. She says as soon as she heard, she got one of the refuge women, Fiona, to go across to find him and the upshot is, he's staying in one of the refuge's emergency rooms for the night and Fiona'll see him onto the train first thing in the morning. Mam offers to go to pick him up but Gayle says no, she'll do it because Tommo sounded upset and it's time she had a proper talk with him.

I go to bed thinking how weird it is that a pair of losers like Benny and Gayle could produce someone as fine as Tommo. Then my mind drifts on to Erin and I have very sweet dreams.

Tommo calls round for me about nine the next night. Neither of us says anything about the Stirling conversation. We just tell each other we look smart and that's that. Crisis over. Time to move on.

The Centre is heaving by the time we arrive. It's a fourteen to seventeen's disco, so it's packed with those who would normally have gone to a club in town but can't get New Year's tickets without ID. Two of the youth leaders, Mick and Karen, are on the door, checking tickets. 'You know there's no drinking allowed, lads?' Mick says, eyeing Tommo.

'What, even water?' Tommo replies.

Mick rolls his eyes. 'Of course there's water.'

'Good,' says Tommo walking off, 'just in case I get dehydrated with all the E's I've just taken.'

'Not funny, Thomas,' Karen calls after us. But I think it is and I laugh like a maniac. I'm feeling great because it's New Year's Eve and I'm at the disco with my best mate who's on form again and at some stage tonight I'm going to dance with Erin Mackiness.

Stiff PK's up on the decks. We know him from soccer—he used to play mid-field for us before he got into music. He's a black dude with those short, knotty dreads in his hair that I'd have if I were black. It's a good look. 'What do you want to do?' I ask Tommo.

He shrugs. 'Nothing planned.' But he's scanning the dance floor, searching for something.

'Want to stay in here or go to the games room?'

'Either.'

'Just tell me, won't you, if it gets too much?'

He turns to me then, and gives me this sad smile. 'I'll survive,' he says, 'thanks.'

There's a shriek from somewhere in the middle of

the dancing and the gang are all over us. Chantal gabbing on ten-to-the-dozen and Erica nodding and 'yerring' behind her in between blowing paper horns in my ear lugs. Chan's talking to me again, now, since the thing with Benny. I tell her she looks nice and her eyes light up. All the others are fussing round Tommo, asking if he's all right and complaining about not being able to drink or smoke and being treated like kids.

I look at them all, birds and geezers I've known since I could wee in the sand pit and I laugh and allow myself to be sucked into their bubble. Erica lets off a load of those party poppers and Tommo and me yell with the best of them. All the time, though, I'm conscious that I'm waiting for Erin. I haven't seen her yet and I know as soon as I do I'll be off because she's promised me a dance and whatever else happens tonight, that is the one thing I have to do.

After a few minutes Tommo breaks away to go to the bogs and I'm left with Chantal bouncing about on one side of me and Erica on the other. 'Why were you so late?' Chantal asks. 'I've got to go at half ten to blinking babysit.'

'He's been making himself look nice for us,' Erica grins, running her fingers up and down my shirt sleeve.

Chantal belts her hand away immediately. 'Don't touch what you can't afford!' she snaps.

'You don't own him, you know!' Erica fires back.

'Shurrup, Erica.'

I laugh and give them both a peck on the cheek and tell them I'm going to look for Tommo.

'Will you come and dance with us soon?' Chan asks.

'No, I've got a date,' I tell her. Her face falls but I'm learning to be honest and direct like Erin and Tommo; it's the only way.

'Sod you then,' she says.

'I'm still here for you whenever you need me,' I tell her over my shoulder.

Tommo's just emerging from one of the cubicles as I go in. I notice him slip something into his pocket and he winks at me. 'What's that?' I ask him, nodding towards the bulge in his jacket.

'Just something to get me through the night, my friend. Want some?'

He shows me the screw-top of something and I shake my head. His drinking worries me. It's not like the rest of us, who get tanked up after two or three. Tommo drinks with—I don't know—commitment. Like a pro. Like Benny. It's weird, isn't it, how everyone gets freaked out about drugs but nobody fusses so much about booze when booze is the worst drug of the lot. I found that out when I looked up cirrhosis on the Net yesterday. 'You'll be chucked out if they see that,' I warn him.

Tommo, naturally, doesn't see it that way. 'You're so straight, Liam. Lighten up, mate.'

Maybe he's right. Maybe I'm being over-sensitive. I need to be as normal with the guy as I can—after all, he won't be the only one smuggling stuff in tonight. Knowing Chantal and Erica they'll have something miniature hidden in their bags to mix with their cans

174

of Coke. And it is New Year's Eve and all that malarkey so if you can't beat 'em, join 'em. 'Don't hog it all, then,' I tell him, holding my hand out for the bottle.

It's brandy. I take a gulp and I can feel it burning all the way down. Tommo has another massive swig after me, then smiles and throws his arms round my shoulders. 'I'm going to be OK, you know. I'm going to be OK,' he tells me.

'Never doubted it.'

'No point thinking about the past.'

'None.'

'Gotta move on.'

'Always.'

'Positive thinking.'

'Yep.'

Tommo looks at me, a bit sad. 'We're thinking of getting a transfer—you know, swapping our house for one somewhere else. A clean break, you know?'

I don't know what to say. So I don't say anything.

We return to the party. The heat from the dance floor is almost nauseating but we edge round towards the speakers where there are some free seats. We sit down and try to have a conversation but it's a waste of time with all the noise. I point out Chantal necking with one of the geezers from Briar Hill flats and we laugh because she's got her hands on his backside and he keeps trying to shift them away.

'It's Taz Cunliffe's brother, isn't it? Ashley? You've

bitten off more than you can chew there, Ashley mate!'
Tommo grins.

'He stands no chance. She's like one of those things
that stick to the bottom of boats when she gets going.'

Tommo doesn't reply. He taps me on the leg and
says, 'Look who's here.'

'Who?'

'Erin—over there. I've been wanting to see her. I have
to say sorry for acting like such a git the other day.
And she's with Katia, so that means you're sorted,
mate.'

'Oh yeah?' I mutter.

What can I say? He's had enough crap in his life
without me telling him to butt out with Erin. It's up
to her, anyway. I remember the smile she gave me in
her house and I pray it meant what I hope it meant.

My guts ache as Tommo jumps to his feet and starts
waving Katia and Erin over. They see us and move
towards us, all smiles and excited. 'I'm glad you're
here,' Erin goes to both of us, 'we don't know anyone
else.' I'm about to offer to show her round when
Tommo touches her on the arm and asks her to dance.
Just like that. No mention of the weather or how she's
doing. Nothing.

'Sure,' she says not even glancing at me.

Without another word, she follows him on to the
dance floor and it's an effort for me to stand there. I
feel sick and realize it's what they call jealousy. Didn't
recognize it at first because I've never had it. It hurts.
Big Time.

Katia's chatting on about something but neither of us can look each other in the eye. Her shoulders are jigging and I know she's dying to dance, too, but it brings back too many memories of what happened last time.

I glance up at Stiff and he sees me and winks. He motions me to come up and see him so I tell Katia and she asks if she can come, too. I don't see why not so we go and rabbit on for a while. I update him on what's happening with the team and Katia seems happy enough to rummage through his vinyls. She pulls out some punk album from hundreds of years ago and goes into great detail about how her mam used to spit at Johnny Rotten or someone. I don't know what she's on about but Stiff seems impressed and shows her some other old stuff and hey presto Stiff PK has a new partner for the evening, presuming his fiancée doesn't turn up.

From here, I can see Chantal and Erica leaving. Chantal waves at me and points at Ashley, who's staggering along behind her, as if to say 'see!' Behind them Tommo and Erin are still dancing but I can't see their faces. I'll be ending up on my own at this rate, like some anorak-type.

I move down to the dance floor and stand on the edge, taking it all in, looking as if I couldn't give a toss about any of it. A couple of birds in tight-fitting dresses glance over but I'm not interested. I lose sight of Tommo and Erin for ages until I go to the bogs and find them sitting on the couch, so deep in conversation they don't even notice me. I'm tempted to sit between them and say 'Oi, come on,' but they look too chummy, too intense. I go back to the dance floor and take up my Mr Cool position, all the time sinking deeper and deeper into my own misery.

Eventually, Stiff's shouting out instructions to everybody about the countdown and Katia screams out for 'Ernie' to join her, which she does. Tommo appears out of nowhere, taps me on the shoulders and says, 'I'm off.'

'What, now?'

'Need some space. Going to walk home—sort my head out.'

'Is Erin going with you?'

He frowns. 'No, why should she be?'

'Dunno.'

Tommo laughs. It's the first proper laugh he's come out with in months. 'You thought I was trying to get off with her, you daft berk!'

'No I didn't!'

'You are so transparent, Droy. I like talking to her, that's all. She was telling me about being in the Queen's Arcade and hating me and I was telling her about being in McDonald's and hating you.'

'A laugh a minute, then.'

'Friendship, mate.'

I think about him leaving the estate and chuck my arms round him. It feels weird, man. I've never hugged the guy before, except on the soccer pitch. 'I love you, Tommo,' I tell him. Another first.

He grins and hugs me back. 'I always knew you were soft, Droy,' he says, eyes glinting, and disappears just as Stiff screams 'Happy New Year, people!'

I go back to waiting. I wait until nearly everyone's split, apart from the do-gooders sweeping litter into black bin liners and Mick trying to calm the caretaker down after he's seen whatever has been done to the bogs. I wait until I see Erin waiting and slowly I walk up to her. She's watching Stiff and Katia snogging the face off each other. 'They'll have to come up for air soon,' I tell her.

She spins round, smiling. 'Hi. I thought you'd left. I looked, but I couldn't see you.'

'I can't go yet. You promised me a dance.'

She frowns. 'I did, didn't I? Bit late now.'

'I don't think so.'

I pull my mam's compilation CD out from my inside jacket pocket where it's been burning a hole all night. 'Side one, track six,' I inform Stiff. I have to tell him three times before he listens.

'I've got to pack up, man,' he says.

'One song won't hurt.'

He obeys, squinting at the titles. '"Never Ever"?' he mutters. The song starts and I'm just glad it's slow, so I can pull Erin towards me and dance with her. Neither of us say a word. We just kind of stand and sway in each other's arms. I am dancing with Erin Mackiness and that's all I ever wanted.

18
ERIN

'I can smell it! I can smell the sea!' I yelled as we bundled off the coach and spilled in one lethargic mass onto the ferry terminal.

No one else seemed overly impressed. Miserable bunch. OK, it was drizzling, a bit. OK, a lot. OK, nobody had slept a wink and maybe, just maybe that might have been because I hadn't stopped talking from the minute we'd stepped onto the coach outside school at 2.00 a.m. to the minute we'd stepped off the coach at 6.00 a.m., so half of them were feeling grumpy and the other half were feeling sleepy but that's enough dwarf jokes . . .

I grinned at Gabriel and pointed out the beautiful white ferry ahead. 'Look, Gabriel, boat—*bateau*. Now remember what Mr Whitehead told us. No running off on your own. We don't want any accidents before we get to Le Havre.'

Gabriel, who had turned into a wet mollusc since meeting Jessica, jutted out his bottom lip and yanked the hood of his anorak further down his long face. 'I'm missing her already,' he complained for the umpteenth time. 'If only I'd known in October how I'd be feeling in April, I wouldn't have signed up.'

'It's only five days,' Hannah said.

'Five whole days without Jess will seem like a life-time. I only see her during the holidays anyway,' the love-struck one continued.

Katia thrust her mobile phone under his nose. 'Ring her and put us all out of our misery. Then put a sock in it.'

Delighted, Gabriel began punching in numbers just as Mr Whitehead started barking orders about following him up the gangway and staying together and taking care not to slip. I obeyed instantly, pulling my rucksack more firmly onto my shoulders and facing the ferry. I felt like a five year old on my first trip to the seaside, pathetically over-excited, but the trip to France had just been such a long time coming, and such hard work getting here, I was determined to savour every second. That's what Dad had said as he hugged me goodbye earlier—savour it, Erin, so I'd started savouring at two o'clock and didn't intend to stop.

I dug deep into my cagoule pocket until my fingers found the edge of my wallet. I grinned to myself. Every euro inside that leather pouch had been scraped together and earned by me. Pocket money, babysitting money, and recently working in Quarashi's now-and-again-when-he-needed-someone money. And I felt so proud of myself that I'd done it.

Something else jutted next to my wallet. Something soft. I pulled and found one of Georgia's favourite beanie babies. 'Oh, look,' I said to Katia as we finally approached the stairway leading onto the deck, 'Georgia said she was going to give me something for good luck to ward off the icebergs. I told her lettuces never hurt anyone. Lettuces—iceberg—get it?'

Katia turned and smiled. 'This is what Darin gave me.' She tugged at her collar to reveal a huge love-bite worthy of any Scrunchie.

'Very subtle, darling,' I told her. 'I take it you're back on again, then?'

'For now,' she said lightly.

Her relationship with Stiff PK, also known as Darin Dean, aged nineteen, had been stop-start-stop-start since New Year. It tended to stop when his ex-fiancée turned up and start again when she bogged off. It wasn't my idea of going out with someone but Katia was never going to be conventional, was she?

Eventually, sixty Year Tens from Adams High assembled on the deck of the ferry, which I noticed for the first time was called the *Lady Diana*. Anything to do with Lady Di always reminds me of her greatest fan, Mrs Droy. I cast my eyes around for Liam. I hadn't seen much of him so far because he had drifted to the back of the coach on the way here and I had been at the front with Hannah because she gets travel-sick on journeys.

I couldn't see him, so concentrated instead on Mr Whitehead. He was scowling at his soggy clipboard, conferring with Mme Crecy and some of the other teachers. The rain was beginning to fall harder now and the normal people had headed straight inside.

'Right, chaps. I want you all to get into groups of between four and six and give yourselves a name. One of us will come round for your group name and assign you to a leader for this part of the trip. OK, quickly now.'

'Couldn't have done that on the coach where it was dry, could he? That would have been far too practical,' Katia grumbled, then told Gabriel he had one second sharp to say goodbye to the wife.

We huddled round to think of a name. 'How about The Crusty Croissants?' Hannah suggested.

'No, no—the Load of Boules,' said Katia, 'or The Madames from Adams.'

'I'm not a madame!' Gabriel protested.

'We've got to keep it simple,' I said. 'What about "The Tables"?'

'The tables? How boring is that?' Katia scoffed.

'It doesn't matter how boring it is. If it wasn't for a table I wouldn't be here and, let's face it, gang, if I wasn't here, how boring would this event be for you lot anyway? Come on!'

Mr Whitehead approached, rain dripping off his nose. 'And you are the . . . ?' he asked, scribbling down our names into an empty box on his page.

'Tables,' I declared firmly.

'Just the four of you?'

'Yes—no.' From the corner of my eye, I spotted Liam, hanging slightly back from the group Mme Crecy was recording. He looked totally fed up. Partly that was his own fault for not being seen dead in a cagoule and therefore being soaked through, partly because I knew Thomas had moved to Scotland last week with his family. Liam hadn't said much about it on the way to school on a morning but I knew he was cut up about it.

'There's five tables,' I corrected, waving for Liam to join us.

'Isn't that what they call a nest of tables?' quipped Mr Whitehead.

'If we laugh at your joke can we go inside straight away?' Katia asked.

Mr Whitehead chewed thoughtfully on the end of his pencil. 'If you laugh at my joke *and* buy me a cappuccino,' he smiled.

'Done!'

The girl with the vampire neck immediately linked arms with Hannah and Gabriel and rushed towards the porthole or whatever doors on ferries are called, ignoring shouts of 'Watch it, cow-bag,' from our fellow Adams High travellers.

Liam stood next to me, staring down from beneath his Raybans. Did he ever stop posing? Answer—no. 'You called, Mackiness?'

'Just wondered if you wanted to be in our group?'

He half-shrugged, half-grinned, 'Why not?'

'Sorted then,' I smiled.

Mme Crecy came clomping up, trying to balance her clipboard with one hand and umbrella with the other. 'Liam!' she said exasperated already, 'are you still one of the Dick'eads, or not?'

Liam and Mr Whitehead exchanged sharp glances.

'Don't look at me! It wasn't my idea,' Liam said in his defence before the question had even been put to him.

'No, miss, Liam's with me,' I said quickly.

'Very well,' Mme Crecy fumed, crossing out his name and returning to the other group, where Mr Whitehead was already having 'words'.

'So, I'm with you, am I?' Liam asked uncertainly, cocking his head to one side.

'Only if you want to be.'

I reached for his hand which was dry and warm, intending only to hold it until we got inside but somehow, I forgot to let go. Well, I couldn't let him loose on the French, could I? Not the way he danced.

Helena Pielichaty (pronounced Pierre-li-hatty) was born in Stockholm, Sweden but most of her childhood was spent in Yorkshire. Her English teacher wrote of her in Year Nine that she produced 'lively and quite sound work but she must be careful not to let the liveliness go too far'. Following this advice, Helena never took her liveliness further south than East Grinstead, where she began her career as a teacher. She didn't begin writing until she was 32. Since then, Helena has written many books for Oxford University Press. She lives in Nottinghamshire with her husband and two children.

www.helena-pielichaty.com